The Unraveling of Reverend G

"RJ Thesman expresses herself so well. She writes beautifully."
~ *Keith Johnson, Johnson County Gazette*

"I really like how RJ Thesman weaves God's messages clearly into the story." ~ *Mary Geisler, Vice President of Finance for a large nonprofit organization.*

"A heartwarming story of family and love. I highly recommend it!" ~ *Charlene Shibel, Director, Home Health and Hospice agencies with a medical center*

The Unraveling of Reverend G

RJ THESMAN

CROSSRIVER

THE UNRAVELING OF REVEREND G
Copyright © 2012 RJ Thesman

For more information on RJ Thesman, please visit her website - www.rjthesman.net

Cover Artwork: Jackie Dix
Cover Design: Tamara Clymer
Printed in the United States of America

To all the caregivers who
so patiently watch over those
who sometimes forget.

RJ THESMAN has been a writer since she flipped open her Red Chief tablet and scribbled her first story. Eventually, she attended college where she earned an education degree and taught at various levels, including short-term missions in Honduras. Thesman is a Biblical Counselor and a Stephen Minister. She has worked as a communications professional in a variety of nonprofits and has served as campus minister to international students. Thesman enjoys teaching writing workshops and helps beginning writers birth their words. She is the mother of an adult son and enjoys reading, gardening and cooking — especially anything with blueberries. Thesman lives in Kansas with her son and an elderly cat. She enjoys hearing from readers at her website *www.rjthesman.net*.

acknowledgments

Once upon a time, a writer woke up with a story. In the process of transcribing that story, several people helped her make it to publication. I am grateful to the following:

My parents, *Henry and Arlene Ediger* — who traveled the roads of dementia and Alzheimer's with courage and grace.

Jaye Davis — who kept asking the question writers love to hear, "What happens next?"

Genie Helm — who listened to the synopsis of the story and didn't once say, "That won't work."

Deb Kemper and *Jewel Weide* — who prayed for the book to be published. I'm sure God will tell Jewel about it in heaven.

The members of *Christian Writers Fellowship* and *Heart of America Christian Writers Network* — who helped me grow.

My personal prayer team — who keep reminding God that I'm still trying.

Julane Hiebert — who offered an honest critique peppered with enthusiasm.

My Lifegroup — who understood when I couldn't join them, because I had to write.

My son, *Caleb* — who answered honestly when I asked, "Is this okay? How does this sound?"

The staff of CrossRiver Media — who believed in the story.

Shanna Groves — who taught me that it's possible to learn Twitter as a second language.

Marcia Norwood — who encouraged me and dared me to believe in the dream.

My marketing team — who helped me make the right contacts and covered the dream in prayer.

And to all those folks who sometimes forget, I love you and I pray someone will discover a cure for Alzheimer's.

chapter 1

As I circled the day on my wall calendar, I pondered other important days in my life: the day I fell in love with Jesus, the day I named my newborn son, the day of my ordination ceremony.

At the moment, the exact days of the week for those events hid in one of my memory blips. But this day, this Tuesday, might forever highlight itself. A Tuesday. A normal day with no special notations on the calendar, except my appointment with Doc Sanders. Today. Tuesday. But a normal day? Probably not. This was the day I had dreaded for so long.

Later, I wondered if Doc felt the same. "Sorry, Reverend G," Doc Sanders said, "but it's time to do something drastic."

"Are you sure? Are you absolutely, positively, without a doubt sure?"

"All the tests verify the diagnosis, besides — I think deep down you know the truth. Shall I call your son? Would you like me to tell him?"

"No. I'll do it. Thanks, Doc."

I lowered myself off the sterile table, wishing I could escape from this particular room on this particular day. How in the world had I grown into such a senseless woman? When God planted the cells of old age in my body, why did he choose the ones that would keep me from dealing with life? For years, I served the Lawton Springs Community Church as their associate pastor and women's minister. Whether I sang in the choir, taught Bible studies or organized women's retreats – my role as minister filled me with joy. People, both inside the church and outside, made appointments for counseling. Well-known for my ability to get to the root of the problem, I suggested practical solutions and fervently prayed.

But lately, my regulars stopped coming or no longer requested my insightful suggestions. I forgot a few appointments and once, I sort of spaced out in the middle of a session. One of the church families struggled with their teenage son. Mother, father and teenager filled the perimeter of my office.

"I just wanta' pierce one ear," the kid said.

"It's sacrilegious to put a hole in your head," his father countered. The two sides debated back and forth while I mentally outlined what I wanted for lunch. I mean, really, in a world of teenage suicide, drugs and sexually transmitted diseases – who cared about one pierced ear?

Suddenly, the room seemed stifling in its silence as everyone stared at me. "So," asked the father, "what do you suggest?"

I leaned forward and said, "Spicy mustard on both sides of the burger and grilled onions. Try it. You'll like it."

After that fiasco traveled around the church membership, one of the elders asked me if I was all right. "Of course," I said. "Are you all right?" But it bothered me, the way he stared at me as if I had salad croutons pasted to my forehead. He whispered to the church secretary on his way out the door. Heaven knows what she told the Bible study ladies who met every third Thursday whether they needed to or not.

I was losing it. Loony tunes in person and in living color. How in the world was I supposed to fulfill my call as a minister when I could barely remember the order of the minor prophets? Was Obadiah first or Nahum? Joel or Amos?

Even worse, I flubbed communion. Maybe I should have changed my plans for the service. Rented Mel Gibson's *Passion of the Christ* and projected it on the south wall of the sanctuary. Instead, I called the deacons together and we fixed all the communion stuff. Big mistake. We could have lived without communion for another week, but that was sour grapes now, literally.

So many Sundays I officiated at my favorite sacrament, prayed over the crackers and the grape juice and tried to help my congregation understand what it meant to remember Jesus. I wanted them to grasp the importance of the sacrament, to stop the craziness of life and focus on the crucifixion for just a few moments. I put a lot of thought and prayer into each communion service, tried to make it fresh and less superficial.

Maybe if we had used real wine and a loaf of bread for that communion service. But the church elders would have vetoed that idea. None of that alcoholic stuff, even though I knew their wives occasionally poured a little beer into the cake batter to keep it moist.

I stood in the pulpit and spoke into the mike. "We eat this symbol of the bread, remembering Jesus as the Bread of Life. He gave his earthly, physical body so that we might live. He suffered incredible pain, because he loved you and me. If you were the only person on earth, he still would have died for you. Remember Jesus."

I waited a few moments while the congregation munched on their crackers.

Oh, Lord. I hope their hearts are full of love for you. I love you, precious Savior.

Then it was time for the grape juice.

"Now, Lord, as we drink this symbol of the wine, we remember how you bled for us. Thank you, Jesus, for giving yourself for us. You let them nail you to that horrible cross where you suffered for six excruciating hours. Thank you for the power of the blood that washes us clean from our sinful thoughts, attitudes and behaviors. Thank you for saving us from past, present and future sins."

The people seemed to concentrate on their juice, probably wondering if it was Welch's or the local generic brand. The solemn chords of the organ lulled us back to that moment, two thousand years ago on Calvary's hill. Even the babies stopped crying. No one sneezed or coughed to relieve the silence. We finished the communion service, then started to recite the Lord's Prayer.

That's when I goofed. We loped along with the memorized words and came to the phrase, "Forgive us our trespasses." But I suddenly forgot the trespass word. It just would not travel the short distance from my brain to my mouth. After fifty million times praying that same prayer, the "T" word floated out of my head and settled somewhere in the cobwebs at the top of the sanctuary.

I stopped speaking while my brain played the *Jeopardy* theme song and tried to locate that one word.

Help me, Lord.

T…something to do with sins…Trouble…nope that's not

it. Tough times…not even close…Time out…maybe. Forgive us our time outs? Impossible. How about, just forgive us when we mess up. Close enough.

But the congregation romped on without me as they repeated the rest of the prayer. When my brain finally kicked into gear and found the word, they were already onto "and the power and the glory forever."

"Trespasses," I said.

Every head in every pew jerked forward. Eyes stared at me. A baby whimpered. Mrs. Simmons in the second row, left side, snickered. That's when I knew for sure I was in trouble. The next morning, I made the appointment to see Doc Sanders.

∽

"Jacob, can you come over for supper tonight? I know it's the last minute, but I need to talk to you, Son. It's important. You and Jessie, please?"

My son, the CFO at the biggest bank in town, never answered the phone. He responded only to voicemails, but he would come. I knew it, and he would bring his bride with him. Jessica. Sweet girl.

I made his favorite meal: enchilada casserole with tortilla chips and Velveeta sauce. Lousy for the arteries. Great on taste. Jacob needed something delicious to help distract him from the bad news I was about to spill. Come to think of it, I also needed something especially tasty. I looked in the freezer and pulled out a blueberry pie.

The phone jangled. "This is Reverend G. May I help you?"

"It's me, Mom. What's up?"

15

"How about your favorite Mexican meal? My place, about 6?"

"Sure, but you sounded so serious on the phone."

"Don't worry about it, Hon. Just bring Jessie and yourself and spend an evening with your old Mom."

"You're not old. I'll pick up Jess after work and we'll be there. See you soon."

I stuck the blueberry pie in the oven and turned up the heat. "Thank you, Mrs. Smith. Old Reverend G never could make a pie crust worth eating, but you've done it for me."

It took me years to train my congregation to call me Reverend G. Cursed by my parents who for some strange reason named me Gertrude, I hated every possible rendering of the name and even any nicknames. Gertie – sounded like a brand of corset-tight girdles that belonged on a Victorian heroine. Trudy — reminded me of the word "truly", mispronounced, and that old Perry Como song, "I love you truly, truly dear." Gert — no way.

The only person ever allowed to give me a nickname was my good friend, Chris. We struggled together through seminary. He helped me survive Hebrew, and I helped him earn a B in New Testament Survey. During seminary, Chris decided to call me Tru. I liked it, as "Tru" reminded me that truth is always better than deception, even better than those tiny white lies. The truth indeed sets us free. So Chris called me Tru, but for everybody else in my congregation, Reverend G worked just fine.

Although I earned my doctorate of theology degree, I hated to be stuck at some university, teaching eschatology all day. I longed to be out in the field, to help people and serve a congregation. So the Lawton Springs Community Church seemed the perfect setting for my gifts. I loved every minute of my work there and the people embraced me as family. I faithfully served them, and they supported me during the hard times. We alternately loved and tolerated each other but knew that together, we represented an integral part of God's family.

Now, I let them down. No longer the energetic, intelligent Reverend G, once a brainiac and summa cum laude — now I forgot how to recite the Lord's Prayer with the proper "T" word. Gone again. What was that word?

I sat at the kitchen table and pulled my Bible onto my lap. *I need something tonight, Lord. Some comfort, before I tell my beloved son this bad news. Give me encouragement, Holy Spirit, wisdom and strength to tell Jacob the truth. As this disease progresses, please don't let me ever lose the joy of hearing your voice. Do not let me forget you. I can't stand it.*

As I flipped through the Psalms, that familiar warmth permeated my soul. God himself, Immanuel, answered my plea and sent me verse after verse of encouragement and joy. Phrases from the pen of King David and copyrighted by the Holy Spirit floated from my soul clear out to my epidermis: "Trust in me, cling to me, I am your refuge." The Comforter held me close as we talked about how to tell Jacob the truth.

Don't let him hate me, Lord, or worry about the weirdo I may become. Don't let me grow into a violent old woman. I can't stand it. And please, I don't want to curse or become a stumbling block to anyone. Help me, please.

"Do not worry. Do not be anxious. Trust me."

The same words I spoke thousands of times in my office to hundreds of counselees drifted back to me. Trusting in God meant believing not only that he could help me, but that he would do it. It meant knowing that God knew the answers before I asked the questions. I challenged my church members to believe, even in the most dire of circumstances. Could I not trust God now when faced with this life-changing situation? Where stood the faith of Reverend G?

I confessed my lack of trust and waited in the silence of the house for that confirming hug in my spirit. For so many years, God as my husband and maker, loved me in secret when no one else could. Faithful again, he slowly and deliciously covered me with a peace I could never describe even during my most prolific sermons. A peace I could only experience and enjoy.

We sat together in sweetness until the smoke alarm reminded me of the blueberry pie.

⌒∽

"Good grief, Mom. What is that smell?"

"Toasted blueberries, I'm afraid, and a blackened crust. You've heard of blackened chicken, right? Well, this is blackened pie crust. I plan to smother it with Ben & Jerry's. You'll love it. I refuse to throw away a blueberry pie."

Jacob tossed his Yankees baseball cap on the table, then grinned. "Okay by me, as long as the casserole isn't burnt."

I set the baked casserole on Jacob's side of the table, knowing he wanted to dig out the first spoonful. After the fiasco with the pie, I stood by the oven for thirty minutes and watched the cheese and tortillas melt together until the timer finally dinged. Perfect. At least one part of the evening smelled like success.

"Have I told you lately that I love you?" I crossed the kitchen and hugged him, then wrapped my arms around Jessie. "And I love you, as well, dear Jessie."

She kissed my cheek, and I smelled her Estee Lauder Beautiful cologne, the only brand she ever wore. I warned Jacob when they dated that he'd better save extra money for every Valentine's Day. Jessie was worth every penny of that cologne. Not every mother-in-law bragged that her daughter-in-love was Teacher of the Year in the second grade and a great match for her son. I felt so lucky to have them both. Especially now.

We set the table together, using my mis-matched Pfaltzgraff and Goodwill patterns. I collected them willy-nilly through the years and focused on the colors of the American southwest. I so loved the terra cottas, the corals and the yellowish-greens. They reminded me of lazy summers in New Mexico when my family traveled to Santa Fe for a week. How I wished I could return to those days, to be young and carefree. We visited the pueblos and read brochures about the history of the Native Americans. On Fridays, we toured the Plaza booths that sported every form of artistic endeavor: pottery, rug weavings, jewelry. One year, my dad bought me a turquoise ring which I cherished.

But now, I couldn't find it. Probably hiding with that "T" word from the Lord's Prayer. Ah, the joy of disappearing into the past and traveling to Santa Fe in memory.

But if I stayed in a mental vision of New Mexico, Jacob and Jessie disappeared from my brain. And Chris. I missed them. Besides, if I lived in the memories of Santa Fe, that included going through puberty again, mentally. Who wanted to relive puberty? Not me — not even for a minute.

Oh, God — please do not let me revert back and regress to puberty. Don't let me act hormonal or get pimples again. I can't stand it.

We held hands. I squeezed Jacob's with my left and Jessie's with my right as I repeated that beautiful prayer from the old Anglican collection: "Lord, bless this food and grant that we may thankful for thy mercies be. Teach us to know by whom we're fed; bless us with Christ, the living bread. Amen."

Hurray for me — the brain remembered a prayer.

"Amen," echoed Jacob and Jessie.

True to form, my son helped himself to a gigantic spoonful of enchiladas while Jessie passed the chips and dip to me. My appetite sandwiched itself between nervous energy and downright fear, but I was determined to stick my fork into the casserole and give it a try. My son needed to see me in somewhat cheerful spirits, in spite of the bad news I had to share.

Come on, Reverend G. Pretend to accept this horrible verdict and move on with courage. That's what mothers teach their children, to persevere, to have courage in the tough times of life. Well, maybe. Perhaps we just lie to ourselves and to our children. Maybe honesty is better — to be blunt about how we feel so that our children see us as we truly are — flawed and scared half to death.

Jessie crunched a chip and then giggled. "One of my kids was so cute today. We studied about Columbus and recited the old poem, 'Columbus sailed the ocean blue in fourteen hundred and ninety-two.' Then Skip followed it with, 'Scooby-dooby-doo.' We all laughed until it was time for recess."

Jacob chuckled and said, "Pass the dip, Jess. This is so good, Mom."

"Glad you like it, Hon. Always a pleasure to have you two join me for supper." I looked across the table and met my son's hazel eyes. How could I possibly convey to him how much I loved him and that crazy cowlick that still sprouted from his sandy head? We fought that thing all through his adolescence and tried every possible haircut, except the Mohawk. The minister's son just could not wear a Mohawk.

"So, Mom…you said you needed to tell us something. What's the deal? Are you going out of state to preach again or lead a women's conference?"

Oh, Lord, if only it were that simple. To travel and preach again — to meet incredible women all over the conference, encourage them in their faith and hold their hands as we pray. Help me, Lord.

"Nope. Not going out-of-town, but you may need to take care of the house for me."

The space between Jessie's eyes creased into an anxious eleven sign. I wanted to disappear behind that forehead and make it all better, but instead, I dipped another chip and took a bite. The silence of the kitchen waited for my explanation.

"What did you two think of last Sunday's service, particularly communion and the Lord's Prayer?"

I caught the furtive look between Jacob and Jessie, the spark of humor in their eyes. "Go ahead. Laugh. It was funny, I agree."

Jessie tried to smooth over the moment. "It was just that you said, 'Trespasses,' so much later than the rest of us, and it came over so loudly through the mike."

"It was great, Mom," Jacob added. "Don't worry about it. People may laugh about it for a while, then they'll forget it. You know how folks are."

"Oh, darlings, I'm not worried about what people may think. I could care less. I'm worried about what precipitated that moment and why it happened."

"What do you mean?" Jessie asked.

I dipped another chip in the Velveeta sauce. Might as well fill my arteries with more cholesterol. It didn't matter what I ate; the verdict remained the same.

"Doc Sanders conducted several tests on me. For several months, I've suspected a problem. Sunday and the communion service was the icing on the proverbial cake. Does anybody want anything else to drink?"

Avoid the subject just a little longer. Pretend to be thirsty. I walked to the sink and poured water into my glass.

When I sat back down, Jacob and Jessie held hands as if they suspected something terrible. Might as well get it over with.

"I've forgotten my keys several times — not just misplaced them, but completely forgotten how to use them. I disappear into a mental coma, sit in the car, wonder why it won't start, and try to stick my fingers into the ignition.

"One day, I found the iron in the freezer. Another time, my best Sunday shoes showed up in the trash can. Even now, I'm not sure where I filed my sermon notes from last week. Maybe you could help me find them."

"We all forget things, Mom. Stress does it to me all the time or even the allergy season in spring. I forget important things when the trees start budding."

"That's right," added Jessie. "It happens to me, too. Sometimes my chemicals get out of whack or my hormones make things fuzzy. Maybe a new medicine will help you feel better."

I shook my head. "I discussed all those arguments with

Doc Sanders — several times. He checked my chemicals and hormones. I have no allergies, and I'm not taking any medicines. Stress is, of course, always a factor. But Doc confirmed the test results and verified them with three other physicians. They all came to the same conclusion. Are you ready for Ben & Jerry's yet?"

"Mom, for heaven's sake. Get to the point. What's the problem?"

I sighed and bowed my head. "It's dementia, possibly early-onset Alzheimer's. Doc suggests that I retire while I can still focus. He thinks I should move into assisted living. He's afraid I might hurt myself, leave the stove on, forget how to drive or — heaven help us — burn the blueberry pie."

Nobody said anything for what seemed like fifteen years. Finally, I looked up and locked into Jacob's eyes. I expected to see compassion or fear, but stared at downright anger.

"That's preposterous. We'll go somewhere else for another opinion. The Mayo Clinic or alternative medicine or something. I'll Google it tomorrow. This is not possible. You're the smartest woman I know. Plus, you're only 62."

"Dementia does not mean I'm stupid. It just means that some of the wires aren't firing right or connecting like they should, and it can happen earlier in life than you might imagine. It's not a death sentence, although it feels like a type of death. And I don't want to go to the Mayo Clinic. We have great physicians right here in Lawton Springs, and Doc Sanders has always been excellent at diagnoses. Besides, I believe in my heart — he's right."

"No. I refuse to accept this. I will not let it happen. You're my mother, and this is not right." Jacob pushed away from the table, stomped out the kitchen door and disappeared into the back yard.

Jessie wiped tears from her cheeks. She touched my hand and said, "I'll go talk to him." Estee Lauder wafted out the door.

I picked up the dirty dishes and carried them to the sink. From the window which I suddenly decided should be cleaned, I watched Jacob pace around the yard. Jessie stood under the oak tree and waited. Wise girl. Let him work it out before you intervene. He needs to analyze everything. Give him time.

Something about the way Jacob walked, hunched over with fists clenched, reminded me of his father. Although Frank died twenty some years ago, the old fear settled in my stomach. I repeated the same words I prayed ever since Frank decided to stop going to AA.

Dear God, please do not let Jacob be like his father. Do not let my son repeat the sins and habits of the past. Keep him healthy, with no desire for alcohol.

Bible verses floated through my soul. "Do not fear for I am with you; do not anxiously look about you, for I am your God. When I am afraid, I will put my trust in you." It took several repeats of my favorite verses before the acid fear left my gut. I reached into the freezer and grabbed the Ben & Jerry's. Might as well help myself to an extra spoonful of Chunky Monkey while the kids stomp down the grass in the back yard.

Hmm — the hollyhocks are pretty this year. Maybe I should collect the seeds and give some to Jessie for their yard. Except I probably won't be living in this neighborhood when the flowers turn to seed, so it's a moot point. Maybe I'll just stand here and enjoy the scarlet blooms while I still possess some of my wits.

Stay on track, old girl. Trust in the Lord for everything, even the memory of flowers. You need what's left of your brain for the next few weeks or however long it takes to settle everything and move. Let Jacob work out the logistics of everything and trust God to take care of you.

Lord, I know that asking "Why?" isn't usually a good idea, but why did it have to be my brain? "Why" is a confrontational word, and ever since the days of Job, you chose not to tell us why things go wrong. I guess you don't have to tell me now. This is just not the way I planned to go out. I never wanted to retire or move into assisted living. Remember? I hoped to work into my eighties, give a great last sermon and then lay down my life for the sake of the Gospel. I really wanted to end up a martyr with an article about my life on the front page of the Lawton Springs Daily Journal. Do I really have to end up drooling into red gelatin at the nursing home?

"Trust me. The question may be 'Why', but the answer is 'Who.' Focus on who I am."

Yeah, yeah. I know who you are – Yahweh, the one true God who knows the end from the beginning. But how do I do this? How do I just turn off a lifetime of ministry and wither away without any purpose day after day? How do I find any significance in this new life?

"Trust me."

Trust you. Okay. I know where you're headed in this conversation. You are sovereign God, and you always have a plan. Somehow, you can help me find a new purpose. But I'm going on record that I don't like this one little bit. Help me through it, Lord.

Footsteps sounded on the deck. The kids were coming back in. Time for more confrontation or further explanation.

I dipped a heaping spoonful of ice cream, but accidentally dropped it in the sink before I could get it into my mouth. Quickly, I put away the carton and tried to smile.

The door slowly opened.

chapter 2

acob engulfed me in a spine-crushing hug. "I'm sorry, Mom. Sorry I went ballistic. I guess I'm mad at God for allowing this to happen. Just the thought of you turning into someone like Grandpa...it's too much to deal with. At the end, he forgot who we were. He forgot how to eat, how to get dressed...he even forgot how to sing, and I loved to hear him sing."

"I know, Honey, and I don't want to be like that either. I apologize already if that's what happens, but let's just take it one day at a time. Okay?"

After another hug from Jacob and then an Estee Lauder smelling one from Jessie, I hoped to make the rest of the evening more enjoyable. Forget about tomorrow and whatever might happen. Just focus on this moment. This one moment. Don't forget the way Jessie smells or the strength of Jacob's hugs. Cache the memory away for that terrible day when reality disappears. Try to help Jacob through it.

"Okay, who wants pie and ice cream?"

"No pie for me," Jacob said.

"Me, neither," said Jessie.

"What? You don't like blackened blueberries? Well, then — how about ice cream? Chunky Monkey."

I reached for the dessert bowls, then searched in the freezer for the familiar Ben & Jerry's box. But it had disappeared. "Hmm, I know the ice cream was right here a minute ago. I sneaked a bite while you kids were outside. Now where did I put that silly thing?"

We took turns looking through the freezer and then the fridge, the top of the cabinet and the microwave. Nowhere. Did I finish it off and put it in the trash? Nope. Not there. A tiny edge of fear gnawed at my stomach. Once again, I forgot how to do something, a simple thing like where to put my favorite ice cream. How does a half gallon of Chunky Monkey just disappear?

"It doesn't matter, Mom. Let's clean up everything and forget about dessert."

"But Jacob, it does matter. It's another sign that I'm losing the last of my marbles. Besides, I really wanted another scoop or two. This is bizarre."

"It's okay," said Jessie, giving my shoulder a pat. "Let's do the dishes and maybe the ice cream will suddenly appear." I didn't miss the look she gave Jacob — sort of like a dear-old-Mom-she's-really-going-bonkers-type-of-look. I swallowed my own despair and wished I could rewind the past hour, like my church secretary when she restored the computer to an earlier date. Rewind. Restore. Find the stupid ice cream.

We worked together as a team, rinsed off the dishes and stacked them in the dishwasher. Jessie washed the heavy casserole dish while Jacob wiped off the table. I swept some crumbled chips out the back door. Then I put all the Tupperware leftovers into the fridge and scanned the shelves once again for that infamous box of ice cream. Where in the world could it be?

This is not good, Lord. Did I put it in my bedroom closet? In the bathroom? How dumb would that be. Who takes ice cream to the bathroom? But then again, who burns the blueberry pie when company is coming? Help me, God. I can't stand it.

Each of us found our favorite chairs on the deck and sipped iced tea. A chorus of cicadas announced the coming evening while a V-troop of geese flew over the backyard on their way to Conway Lake. Jacob tilted his head back and watched them disappear toward the end of my cul-de-sac.

Memorize Jacob's face and hide this moment in a deep pocket of my soul — in the mother pouch that cannot be touched by this insidious disease. Remember how Jacob looked when the last of the sun's rays touched the golden flecks in his hair. Memorize the freckles on his nose that we called "angel kisses" when he was a toddler. Don't forget this moment. It will not come again.

God, please do not let me become like Grandpa, a gentle man who turned into a violent, cursing skeleton. Please, God, don't let me do that to Jacob. Let me die right now. I'd rather be dead than to leave my son with such horrid memories.

"So, Mom, why don't you come live with Jess and me? We're in agreement. We'd love to have you."

"Absolutely," Jessie said. "I'm off during the summers, so you would be no problem during those three months. The rest of the time, we'll work something out, get some of your friends to stop in every day. Please say, 'Yes.' We'd love to have you."

Memorize the faces. This is a special moment in our family history when I still have most of my wits and know how to respond. Remember the kindness of my children and try to return the same grace to them.

I shook my head. "You're both wonderful to even think

about such a thing, but I promised myself years ago, after Frank died…" I raised my right hand in a Girl Scout salute. "I promise I will never be a burden to Jacob and his family."

They both grinned. "At the beginning of your marriage, you need time together, without a crazy woman in the house. And as much as I hope it doesn't happen, I could become a withering version of myself — like Grandpa. If I do, I apologize already."

"No, darlings. I've already decided where I want to live. Cove Creek has always been my favorite assisted living place to visit and minister to the residents. Throughout the years, I've led countless Bible studies at Cove Creek. The staff is wonderful and the rooms spacious, plus it never smells like some of the other places where I served. I know some of the people already, but of course, the residents keep changing in number, and I'll meet new people all the time because I'll forget meeting them the day before. Get it? Forget I met them yesterday."

I tried to laugh, but it sounded and felt hollow. Neither Jacob nor Jessie laughed with me, so I cleared my throat and blundered on. "I have some money in savings, plus, I'll get a discount for being a minister. We can sell the house or rent it out to a nice single mom and her children. Then there's the M&M fund, of course."

"M&M?" Jessie asked. "What's that?"

Jacob reached for her hand. "Ministers and Missionaries. It's a fund our church keeps to help folks when they retire. Otherwise, some of them would live in virtual poverty. They spend their lives serving others and end up with no pension and no investments. Most of them never even owned their own home, so the church developed the M&M account. We organize fundraisers for it every year and take a big offering on Labor Day weekend. Mom gets a percentage from that fund."

"What a great idea," said Jessie. "I sometimes forget how fortunate I am to have a piece of the teacher's retirement fund that grows every year."

"Yes, dearie. Hang on to that money and let Jacob help you with any investments. He's a whiz kid at math." I swatted a mosquito and secretly wished it would inject me with malaria. Maybe I could die of jungle fever and avoid this entire situation.

How about that, God? Could we end this conversation with a nasty bite and a terminal diagnosis? Help me, God, to stay upbeat for Jacob's sake. Help me or take me to heaven, one or the other. Please.

Jessie's face brightened. "I know. Let's have a giant garage sale. I love garage sales. We could put all our stuff and my mother's stuff and all your stuff together and create a giant sale. Invite the church, and put an ad in the paper. I'll tell everybody at my school, and darling, you can invite the people from work." Jessie pecked Jacob on the cheek.

I clapped my hands. "Great idea. I like it. None of my furniture is worth much. It all came from Goodwill or other garage sales, but maybe somebody can use it. The only thing I really want to keep is one bookcase for all my Bibles and commentaries and, of course, my angel collection. I have to keep my angels."

Every year at Christmas, I bought a new angel to hang on the tree. The year Jacob was born, I bought a blue angel with a "Jacob" label. Chris added to my collection when he bought an angel to celebrate my ordination, a small cherub that held a Bible. The ladies from the church auxiliary found out about the collection and added to it each October on Pastor Appreciation Sunday. Then Jacob caught on and bought one every Mother's Day. He gave me a white one with a flowing robe on the day he married Jessie. I probably had 100 angels that I hung on the tree and displayed around the house each Christmas.

The angel collection would probably bring a fat price on Ebay and help with some of the coming expenses, but not if I could help it. Nope. I was not ready to sell them yet. Too many memories and far too many years associated with those angels. I would agree to retire, stop driving and move from my house, but I was not giving up my angels. Not until I had to.

Jacob stretched his legs. "You know what, Mom. I just might be able to salvage some of that pie. Do you mind?"

"Of course not. I'll stick a piece in the microwave and warm it up. Some for you, Jessie? No? Okay, one piece coming right up."

I walked back into the kitchen where I cut a generous slice of the unfortunate pie for my boy, but I had run out of paper plates. So I walked to the pantry where I knew another package of paper plates waited. One thing I always loved about my old house was the enormous pantry. Jacob and I used to joke that he could park his bicycle in there. Jacob...bicycle... now what did I need in the pantry? Oh yes, paper plates.

But when I opened the pantry door, I wanted to scream. In the middle of my tea bins, neatly alphabetized between hibiscus and jasmine, sat the ice cream. Brown and white droplets puddled on the floor.

I stared at the latest evidence of my fading memory and shouted, "Oh, no."

Jacob ran into the kitchen with Jessie close behind. Without a word, Jessie reached for paper towels and started to mop up the mess. Jacob wrapped me in a bear hug and held me until I stopped shaking. "It's okay, Mom. I didn't want ice cream anyway."

"It's not okay. It's another sign I'm a demented mess. I'm starting to act just like Grandpa, and I don't want to. This is terrible."

"I know. Shhh. It's okay. We'll work through it. I'll help you."

"I'm sorry. I apologize already if I do more stupid things. Please don't hate me for what I may become. I don't want to be a burden to you."

"Never. Ever. I love you and always will — no matter what. Remember what you always told me: 'It's not so much what you do, but who you are.' You're my mom, and I'll help you. We'll make it through. It'll be okay."

My wonderful son, now a young man, held me the way I used to hold him. Back then, I shooshed him into silence and comforted him through the hard times. The roles now reversed, and I felt grateful for the Jacob he had become, but still afraid for myself. Sure, he said nice things now, but what would happen when I reverted into a blithering idiot, medicated or strapped into bed? What if Jacob left work early just to come visit me at Cove Creek and I didn't even know who he was? Would that destroy his tender heart?

God, please. Today it was ice cream. What will it be tomorrow? Please, God. Do not let me forget my beloved son. I'm begging you. Let me die right now. I can't stand it.

⌁

The Saturday morning of the garage sale held the promise of a perfect Kansas day. God's choice of sunrise colors included a turquoise background with peek-a-boo rays of golden yellow. My zinnias bloomed in the flower beds — a

33

good start for the coming summer season. Yellow zinnias always cheered me. I hoped they would bring joy to whomever decided to rent the house.

Jacob posted flyers about renting the house and advertised for a single mom who needed a break in her housing budget. We decided to look first in my own congregation, but secretly — I hoped to rent the house to a woman who didn't already attend church. A practical way to reach out to the community and help a family in need, financially and spiritually.

Lord, let her see Christ in us and be encouraged by your love.

I remembered the struggles of single parenting. After Frank died, people in the church helped me with plumbing or electrical needs. Some of the deacons regularly changed the oil in my car. Filled grocery sacks mysteriously appeared on my porch. Those acts of practical love encouraged me during sad days.

Now, renting to another single mom represented payback; another layer of goodwill to someone in need. At least something good might germinate from my dementia.

Yes, Lord. Let it be.

I stood on the front porch, sipped my green tea and watched a stray cat chase a robin.

"Fly away," I warned the bird, "before you get dementia and forget how to search for worms."

Oh, Lord, let me join that robin and escape this mess. What is that Bible verse? "Oh, that I had wings like a dove. I would fly away and be at rest." Yea! I remembered the whole thing.

It wasn't that I dreaded the garage sale. Always a good idea to de-clutter, but it was just the principle of the situation. Once everything sold, there was no turning back. As my bridges of ministry and home burned, I faced early retirement and a new location. Who knew what lay on the other side? How in the world could I continue to serve God in my demented state?

Ever since I turned sixteen, I knew God wanted me to be a minister. He underlined my call with John 15:16, "You did not choose me, but I chose you and appointed you, that you should go and bear fruit." My master's in divinity and doctorate in theology gave me the credibility to use my leadership gifts, but the male-dominated field made it tough to swim upstream.

"Are you absolutely sure you want to follow this career path?" my counselor asked.

No doubt in my mind or my heart. I loved every moment of seminary training and quickly found a progressive church that wanted more females on their staff. Surely God had not deleted my call even while he allowed dementia into my brain. I wanted to serve through however many years God printed on my timeline, but what would that look like as a resident in assisted living?

Show me, Lord. As long as some of my brain cells operate, please let me be an example of your love. Do not let me waste away into oblivion or forget who you are. Do not let me lose your voice.

"Trust me. Don't be afraid."

I smiled as the divine whisper instructed me with the same words I had heard a million times. *Don't be afraid. Trust. Are we still going over the same territory, Lord? Once again, I'm afraid and learning how to trust you more. Haven't I learned that lesson by now? How many years until I automatically trust? Please be patient with me.*

The robin perched on a branch of my redbud tree and squawked at the cat below. Maybe I should try the same thing. Squawk at the fear and the unknowns that tried to entrap me. Repeat encouraging Bible verses while I still remembered them. Believe I could fly away at any time and escape worry, just by focusing on the God who created that turquoise sky.

Jacob's black Mustang pulled into the drive. He jumped out, balancing his Starbucks cup and the cash drawer he prepared for the sale.

"Good morning, sweet boy. I'd offer you some green tea, but I see you already have your poison."

"Yep. Black and plenty strong. Jess is coming later with some muffins she baked for a morning snack. I've got her mocha latté in the car. Open the garage door, please, and I'll set this cash drawer down."

I skipped down the steps, glad that my body still felt limber, even if my brain seemed a little rusty. After I punched in the code, the garage door lifted, revealing all the treasures we had gathered the night before and arranged on tables inside the garage — an odd assortment of almost antiques, junky piles of mismatched dishes and paperbacks we read a hundred times. Jessie made fancy little stickers on her computer for the price tags. Not the greatest estate sale in the world, but we owned lots of stuff to interest a variety of people. The garage smelled like a mixture of oil and the air freshener we sprayed everywhere.

"Folks will be coming soon," I said. "In fact, here's a customer now."

My neighbor to the north adjusted his John Deere hat and strolled into the garage. "Howdy, ma'am. Got any tools for sale?"

"I think so. Over in the corner. Jacob emptied out my hardware drawer last night and marked everything reasonably. Help yourself." Another sip of the green tea, and I felt ready as ever to meet and greet. Dealing with people was always one of my strongest gifts.

Soon the garage filled with neighbors as well as strangers. Some of the church people trickled in with sad faces. Obviously, the gossip grapevine worked overtime. Everyone seemed to know about my predicament.

"Sorry to hear about your retirement, Reverend G."

"We sure will miss you."

"You've always been my favorite minister."

A gray Buick parked near the redbud tree, and I recognized the vehicle. Mrs. Simmons, the one person in my congregation I never seemed to please. As if on cue, the robin flew away. Mrs. Simmons rearranged her arthritic bones as she stumbled out of her car.

Throughout the years, Edna Simmons regularly wrote letters to the church board and asked for my resignation for one reason or the other. One year, she sent a letter because I missed the Ladies Auxiliary craft luncheon, but I had a strong alibi. Just as I walked into the church that day, one of the elders tried to adjust the Christmas tree in the foyer. He fell into the bulletin rack and made a terrible mess. I drove him to the emergency room and waited while they X-rayed his obviously broken ankle. My inscription with a blue Sharpie on his cast read: "God bless this foot and all five toes." It seemed much more important to care for an injured elder than to support the craft luncheon and feed my face with hot chicken salad. But Mrs. Simmons didn't see it that way.

Another year and with another letter, she complained that I wore leather pants to the youth group car wash. "Too risqué for a church leader," she wrote. "Is Reverend G trying to show off her figure?" Heaven forbid anyone should realize I had a cute tushy.

One busy Monday, she sent me an email, complaining about my hairstyle. "We more mature women," she wrote, "should never wear our hair long. Now that you are graying, it makes the congregation feel that their women's minister is out-of-date. Have you considered the new blunt cuts?"

How could I be out-of-date and wear leather pants at the same time? I argued with myself in front of the mirror for about five seconds, then wound my gray hair on top of my head and secured it with my favorite purple clip. My reply email said, "Thank you so much, Mrs. Simmons, for your fashion advice. I appreciate your expertise. However, I believe the Lord likes my hair just as it is." That was the last email I received about my hairstyle.

Que sara sara, I told myself. Forgive, even when you cannot forget. Maybe Mrs. Simmons planned to buy a lot of my sale stuff today and ease her conscience. I tried to ignore her and let Jessie show her everything on the tables.

We stayed busy, sold our junk and talked to people until noon. Jacob negotiated with some of the church members who wanted "something that Reverend G owned." One of my grandmother's doilies that I kept on the sofa brought five bucks — probably a bargain in the antique world. A portrait of Jesus once hung over my piano. Jacob sold it as a companion piece with the piano itself. Some little girl in the neighborhood wanted to start lessons. I felt excited for her, but a little emotional as I remembered refinishing that old upright and gluing white plastic covers on the keys. It seemed like an era ended as pieces of myself traveled out the garage door and piled into car trunks.

Jessie drove to Sonic and brought us lunch, my favorite cheddar peppers and a Route 44 cherry lime-aid. I knew I'd have to pee in about three minutes, but I sipped that tart, sweet drink anyway. Hopefully, Jessie would help me remember how to get to my own bathroom.

As I finished my last cheddar pepper, a familiar white Caddy rolled through the cul-de-sac. Good old Chris — come to encourage me, no doubt.

He parked near the mailbox, then unrolled his six foot and more frame from behind the steering wheel. My heart flipped over — twice — as he strolled up the driveway, his eyes shining friendship.

"Hi there, you old rascal," I said, waving from the shade of the garage.

"Tru, great to see you. You're looking mighty feisty for a woman who's selling her household goods."

"Oh, you know what they say. One man's junk, another man's treasure. I decided to share my junky treasures with the entire city."

Chris sneaked a kiss on my cheek, then looked soberly into my eyes. "What's this I hear about you leaving the ministry? The congregation will feel lost without you."

"They'll get used to it. Some youngster fresh out of seminary will take over and wow everyone with great sermons and a fresh outlook on life — you know, revitalize the entire church."

He picked up a wooden spoon and whacked at a fly on the table.

"Missed," I said. "Nice try."

Jacob slapped the cash box shut, then stood to offer Chris his hand. "Haven't seen you for a while, Dr. Jacobs. Everything going all right?"

"Sure. Just busy, as usual, and fighting a little arthritis. Do you mind if I steal your mother for a while? I thought we might take a drive."

"No problem. We're closing up here. Jess and I can finish everything. Okay with you, Mom?"

"Of course. Just let me jog inside for a minute and grab my purse." I knew I'd better visit the bathroom or one pothole dip would result in a gusher.

We drove along Conway Lake, then parked in front of the Boy Scout campsite. A young couple walked hand in hand, occasionally sneaking a smooch or two. Wildflowers bloomed near the shoreline while butterflies flitted among the coneflower blooms.

"Let's take a walk," Chris said. By the look he gave me when he opened my door, I knew I was in for a debate, but I wanted to avoid it as long as possible.

"What a beautiful afternoon! Thanks for bringing me out here, Chris. Look at the geese over by the spillway. I wonder if they're the same troop that flew over my deck the other night. How did God ever plant inside them the knowledge to make such a symmetrical V?"

"You really want to talk about creation? I captured you on purpose, Tru. Now spill your guts. What's really going on?"

chapter 3

*C*hris always got right to the point. I tended to dance around our conversations for a while, searching for just the right words. But this time, I felt like telling the truth. Chris was my best friend, and together we survived several types of hell.

I confided in Chris when Frank stumbled home, drunk out of his mind. Several times throughout the years, Chris hurried to my home and helped me throw Frank in the shower, then dress him for bed. Chris even cleaned up Frank's vomit and held my hand in the ER when Frank chunked open his head after he fell against our dresser.

For my part, I reciprocated by helping Chris deal with Polly's death. His beloved wife of thirty-two years suddenly discovered a breast lump. Within two weeks, she suffered through a biopsy and a mastectomy, then heard the horrid diagnosis, "We can't get it all." Chemo reduced her to a pale skeleton while the pain of radiation destroyed her spirit. Thirty-two years almost stretched to thirty-three, but Polly died one week before their anniversary.

They had no children, so I picked out Polly's last clothes and helped Chris make the arrangements. When I officiated at the funeral, I barely choked out the eulogy. "We all met in college. Polly was a beloved friend, a beautiful woman, and the heart and soul of Dr. Christopher Jacobs."

I avoided looking at Chris during the funeral, just as I avoided his dear face even now. He had aged well, with shining white hair that flowed past his shirt collar. Both of us secretly wanted to be hippies during the turbulent sixties. We campaigned together for Bobby Kennedy and grieved when he died. Neither of us tried pot although we discussed it. We knew we were headed for seminary, and the phrase, "Attempted to inhale weed" might not look good on our resumes. So instead of any radical rebellion, we clung to our long hair, my leather pants and the tattoo I knew Chris sported under his polo shirt. His students somehow found out and boasted that their favorite professor's chest bore the title of the Beatles' hit, "Let It Be."

If only we Christians would let it be when we found ourselves in times of trouble. Most of us at Lawton Springs Community Church wanted to mirror those always-trusting-God type of people. We preached and lived with strong intentions until life sent us a clod of reality. Then we gritted our teeth, flexed our spiritual muscles and marched forward with all the faith we could muster. My dementia definitely represented a clod of reality. I just needed to trust God, believe he would help me through it and tell Chris the truth.

I sat on one side of a picnic table while Chris balanced me out on the other side. The geese disappeared to the other side of the spillway. A slight breeze ruffled tiny waves on the lake. I stared at those waves, wondering how to best explain things. No time like the present.

"Remember when we visited the nursing homes as part of our community service training in seminary? How we felt so sorry for those poor demented souls and wanted to help them. At the same time, we felt grateful we weren't trapped within those walls, waiting to die? We just drove away and came back the next week."

"Of course, I remember. You were always great with the residents. You held their hands and patted their heads like little puppy dogs. They loved you. What's that got to do with selling your household goods and early retirement?"

"Because I'm going to become one of them. Doc Sanders says I have a form of dementia, maybe early Alzheimer's — or as I like to think of it, Sometimer's. I don't forget all the time; in fact, sometimes, I'm quite lucid. I just forget some of the time. Get it? Sometimer's."

"Not funny. Alzheimer's? I don't believe it. Have you asked for a second opinion? Sanders could be wrong, you know."

"He's done several tests and consulted with various professionals. Yes, it's true. I've already sorted through all the arguments and all the other possibilities with Doc. Oh, Chris — I hate this. I do not want to become a vegetable and drool all over my purple nightie. And I'm even starting to pop out curse words. Never in my life have I done that. I don't even know where those words come from. How does that happen?"

Chris reached across the table and took my hands in his. Such big, masculine hands. Warm and strong. My friend Chris — bigger than life in so many ways. Big hands, big heart, gigantic bass voice, but gentle and sweet when he needed to be. Like now. I knew he hurt for me. I felt his grief on my side of the picnic table.

"You're sure about this drastic change? Retirement and a move all at the same time? Doc can't give you some type of supplement? Some of the new meds that are supposed to be so great?"

"He says no, not right away. It's progressive and I'll only get worse. The deed is done, Chris, and I move into Cove Creek next week. I already do stupid things and make a fool of myself. Last week, I put ice cream in the pantry — Chunky Monkey, no less. This morning I forgot which channel to push for the reruns of "Seventh Heaven," and that's my favorite show. Doc is right. I do need to retire and get out of the pulpit, even though it breaks my heart to leave. Now's the time — before I do anything more ridiculous — like try to officiate another communion service."

"Just because you forgot one word of the 'Lord's Prayer?'" A tiny grin lifted Chris's white moustache.

"It was funny, wasn't it? Trespasses. I hope I never forget that word again." Then the reminder of that Sunday flooded back into memory, and I giggled. Chris joined me and soon we shared memories that made us laugh even harder. It felt so good to be with him, like a toasty marshmallow in a cold junior high camp meeting. Chris always helped me survive, even during the hardest times. One of his greatest gifts included encouragement, sprinkled with laughter.

We chatted about everything except my condition for a couple of hours, then my stomach rumbled. Chris heard it clear on the other side of the table. "So, Madame Minister with Sometimer's, would you like a burger or something?"

"Actually, we ate Sonic hamburgers for lunch. How about a pizza?"

"Perfect. I haven't had pepperoni for ages. There's a new place on the west side of town. How about we check it out?"

"Fine with me, but I should call Jacob so he won't think I've lost my way home and I'm doddering somewhere on the highway. May I borrow your cell phone? Mine disappeared. I hope it's not in the pantry."

We stood up and walked back to the Caddie. Chris gave my shoulder a squeeze as I slid into the passenger seat. I wanted to cry at the thought that I might forget this incredible friend and this beautiful afternoon at the lake. Remember these moments. Remember our conversation and the way Chris's hand felt in mine. Remember two souls who talked across the picnic table.

Remember this moment. Memorize the way Chris walks in front of his car, his muscular arms, those broad shoulders. Remember all the good times with Chris and Polly. Don't forget how Chris brings the joy of God to every room he enters. Even on this beautiful spring day, remember how Chris made it better.

He maneuvered the car through the parking lot and onto the highway while I dialed Jacob's number. Thankfully, I punched the numbers in the right sequence. Jessie answered with a soprano, "Hello."

"Hi, Sweetheart — I expected your hubby's voice, but I'll talk to you instead. Chris and I are going out for pizza. I'll be home in a little while. How's everything going?"

"Okay, but there isn't much left inside the house. We sold the last of the furniture to a guy who buys stuff for the Habitat Restore. You do have a single bed in your bedroom and of course, all your personal stuff. I made up the bed for you."

My heart ached a little at the idea of all the changes ahead. "Thanks, dear, for all you've done today. We can talk tomorrow about the final arrangements. I love you."

"Love you, too. I'll tell Jacob you called."

Nothing left, Lord. Is this what it means to die to self so completely that nothing of this earth matters anymore? Just going on record here, Lord. I don't care that much about all the stuff

45

in the house. I can't take it with me anyway. Just never let me lose you. That would be the worst tragedy of all.

∽

"Nice place," said Chris, as we settled into a booth. The waitress came over with her pad and pen.

"What'll ya' have?" she asked as she clicked her pen.

"Half and half," said Chris. "Pepperoni on my half and for the lady…"

The waitress looked at me as I tried to remember my favorite pizza flavor. Something Jacob hated, but the answer hid somewhere between my brain and my tongue. It was a "trespasses" moment all over again. "Uhm, I'll have, uhm — do you have a list somewhere?"

"I think the lady would like ham with cream cheese and pineapple. Right?"

Tears welled up as I realized Chris had rescued me. I nodded and reached in my purse for a Kleenex, but couldn't find one. I always carried a packet of Kleenex to give to anyone I ministered to. People cried all the time. Now my packet of Kleenex had disappeared. Probably waiting for me to find it in the pantry. Chris grabbed a napkin and handed it to me.

"See what I mean, Chris? I can't even remember my favorite pizza. Ham with cream cheese and pineapple. How hard is that to remember?"

"So, we all have lapses of memory. I took care of it. We're okay."

"No, we're not okay. At least I'm not. I'm so scared, Chris."

He took a sip of his Coke and cleared his throat. "I won't throw any platitudes at you. I'm sure you don't want to hear them. You know all the Bible verses about trusting God, about letting him take care of you no matter what happens. It's true, you know. You can trust him. But God isn't the only one on your side. Remember, you and I are lifelong friends, and I'll help you any way I can. I know you'd do the same for me."

"Thanks. Yes, I would." Someone went to the karaoke bar and started to sing. She wasn't very good, but a few couples jumped up. "Let's dance."

"Huh?"

"Come on, Chris. For old times' sake. Who knows when I'll forget how."

It was a peppy number. We improvised a few steps and covered the entire floor twice. Other couples joined us until we started knocking elbows and hips. Trickles of sweat appeared on Chris's forehead, and I felt perspiration under my armpits. "Enough," he finally said and guided me back to our table just as the pizza arrived.

We finished our food in no time, then watched the younger set do a slow dance. Remember this moment, I told myself. The taste of our pizza, the way we danced together, Chris across the table from me. Remember ham, cream cheese and pineapple.

"Do you know what I'm most afraid of, Chris? It's not health issues or moving to a new place or meeting new people. Heck, if I keep forgetting things, I'll meet new people every day. At least they'll seem new to me. Get it?"

"Got it. I guess that's a good attitude to have. Every day a new day. Every person a new experience."

"Right, so that's a positive. But what if I lose contact with God himself? If I no longer hear his voice, recognize his whisper or remember Bible verses? What if I can't find Ecclesiastes any more or Hebrews or Psalms? I can't stand it."

"You've always had an amazing ability to hear from God and to discern what he says about decisions that need to be made. I envy that type of intimacy with the divine." Chris patted my hand. "He won't leave you, Tru. He never leaves us, never forsakes us."

"Don't patronize me, pal. How do you know that? God's sweet voice has been real to me ever since I gave him my heart. His words helped me through a difficult marriage and all the challenges of ministry. But if I can't hear God or recognize him, I'll be lost. I'd rather be dead. I will be dead without his voice, spiritually and emotionally dead."

The kids on the dance floor gyrated to the beat of the music, but I suddenly hated their youth and energy. How lucky they were, with no clue how quickly life galloped past.

Enjoy yourselves now, young ones. In a few short years, age will knock at your door to hand you diminished brains and shriveled muscles. As shadows of your former selves, you will look like us – with arthritis in your elbows and brown spots on your hands.

I slid out of the booth and started for the door, but where was it? Chris paid the bill while I circled the dance floor and bumped into three kids. Then I heard Chris behind me. "Wait up, Tru. Slow down." He caught up to me, grabbed my arm and steered me outside.

"Now do you understand?" I shouted. "I'm loony. I couldn't find the door and where are we anyway?"

"We're on our way home, Tru, and I'm here. Hold on to me." He pulled me against his chest, and I felt his heart beating. Warm. Steady. Trust-worthy.

"Thank you. Thank you," I mumbled into his shirt, wanting to stay there forever.

We rode in silence toward the growing sunset. God selected an azure shade of blue to blend in with the gray promise of an early thunderstorm. Lightning outlined the biggest cloud, and I rolled down my window to hear the bass drums of thunder. I leaned my head into the breeze and smelled the sweetness of the first rain drops.

"Thank you for the pizza, Chris. Delicious. Please don't hate me for making a scene back there. I don't know why I did that."

"Hate you? That was the funniest thing I've seen in a long time. A tiny woman with gray hair streaming down her back, runs around the tables and searches for the door. We must have been a sight! You sprinting around the dance floor while I tried to catch you, slowed by my trick knee. Did you hear the people cheer when I finally grabbed you?"

I punched Chris in the ribs and laughed. Good old, Chris. He always found the joy in every situation.

He pulled the Caddie in front of my house and slid the gearshift into park. Someone left the porch light on, and a glow shimmered behind it. My kitchen light, illuminating the now empty rooms. "Here we are," Chris said. "Let's have pizza again sometime when I can spirit you away from Cove Creek."

"Okay. When is it I'm going there?"

Chris leaned over and pecked my cheek. "Jacob will let you know. Don't worry, Tru. I'll always be around to help you escape whenever you feel afraid."

"Just as long as I don't escape from my brain and forget everybody I love."

∽

I stood on the porch and waved good-bye, then slowly

opened the front door. Although Jessie warned me, the house looked completely different — like a scene in a movie when criminals break in and steal everything. The almost-empty living room held only one bookcase with my rows of Bibles and commentaries keeping each other company. I ran my hands over their spines: *The Living Bible, Matthew Henry's Complete Concordance, The New American Standard* leather bound edition. How I loved my books! How much longer would I be able to read and understand the incredible words printed within? I sat on the floor, yoga style.

Impressions from the sofa, the coffee table and the piano legs dimpled the carpet where they stood for years. I plunged my fingernails into the grey shag, and a tiny wisp of dust escaped. Obviously, the carpet needed a good cleaning. I imagined Jacob would replace the whole mess while Jessie helped him find just the right color and style to give the entire room a facelift. My wonderful children.

Be grateful. Don't worry about tomorrow. Finish off the day with a snack.

In the kitchen, an empty space mocked me where my table and chairs once stood. Just a week ago, Jacob, Jessie and I sat around that table and discussed my diagnosis. The microwave stood in the corner, secure on an old cart I once found during dumpster diving. Jacob and I used to scour the neighborhoods for the best furniture leftovers when kids left the campus for summer break. Then we carted our treasures home to clean, paint or repair them. We learned all about repurposing furniture, long before it became a popular show on HGTV. Jacob's bedroom furniture came from the dumpsters, as well as two of the kitchen chairs and the microwave cart.

How can this be, Lord, that life has changed so suddenly?

One moment, my son and I hunt for treasures — the next day, it seems, we give them away. Truly, the things of this life that we collect and store are only temporary, but oh, the memories associated with them. The sweet, dear memories. Why did I come into the kitchen, Lord? A snack, that was it, but I guess it doesn't matter now. I'm not really hungry. Nothing matters.

In my bedroom, the dresser accessorized one wall while a twin bed — Jacob's old bed — stood perpendicular to the nightstand. Someone bought my old double bed. Good riddance. The mattress had exceeded its expiration date and the frame held itself together with duct tape. Maybe the Habitat people could somehow restore it.

An antique star-patterned quilt now dressed the twin bed, turned down to reflect purple and white gingham sheets. Waiting for me on the pillow sat a lonely Hershey's kiss – dark chocolate. Bless Jessie's heart. She thought of everything.

I perched on the edge of the bed, sucked on the chocolate and slipped off my shoes. Pale spaces on the walls shadowed the patterns of the family pictures that once hung there. I searched those blanks for my favorites, the collage of Jacob's graduation photos and an eight by twelve of the wedding party when Jacob and Jessie married. Like sentinels simultaneously announcing the past and the present, those photos now stood in a box next to the dresser, ready for the move to Cove Creek.

I slid to my knees beside the bed. *So here we are, God, just you and me in an almost empty house. Help me let go of the leftovers of life and feel your comfort in my heart. Please be with me. Send grace for tonight and the nights to come. Bless my loved ones and somehow prepare me for the move to Cove Creek. Show me how to serve you there, to be an example to the other residents.*

God, I'm going to be a resident, one of those people I once served. I never thought my life would come to this, but you knew about it, before I was born. You saw this moment and designed enough grace for me to deal with it. Thank you, God. Help me.

Tears slid down my face and watered the calico prints on the quilt. A montage of framed memories filtered through my soul — Frank and I trying to discuss finances while his tongue, numb from another drinking binge, slurred the words; Jacob sitting on my bed discussing his college plans; hundreds of moments when I knelt at this spot and prayed for people in my congregation. The congregation I no longer served.

Without taking off my clothes, I slid under the quilt and pulled it up to my chin. A chocolate whiff from the Hershey's kiss greeted me as I lay my head on the pillow and prayed to dream of something other than an empty house and an aching heart.

∽

The church gave me a grand send-off — lots of beautiful cards and a money tree with dollar bills tied to each branch. Jessie announced that she would put the cards into a memory scrapbook. Jacob and his calculator took immediate charge of the tree, adding up the amounts to help with my first month's bills and moving expenses.

Years ago, I made Jacob the executor of my estate and signed a durable power of attorney. A great decision, while I still had all my brain cells. Such a bright mind — that boy of mine. Neither of us anticipated how soon Jacob would need to take control of the finances. Sometimes, we do it right. God foreshadows the decisions of life and leads us in the right direction, then we follow him.

In the fellowship hall, old photos of my years in ministry filled the tables: a Christmas concert when I played the bells, a women's Bible study at my now empty home, the communion service during the infamous "trespasses" moment. A guestbook lay open for everyone to sign their names: "A tribute to the many lives Reverend G has touched," said the chief elder. But I wondered. Was the guestbook with its various cursive signatures a gentle reminder when I forgot all the people I once served? We needed to paste faces beside those signatures. Maybe Jessie could add that to the scrapbook.

Lord, help me remember to ask Jessie about the faces. Don't let me forget. Faces. Signatures. Scrapbook.

Another table included plates of cheesecake with bowls of various toppings: chocolate shavings, blueberries, strawberries and even some gummy worms for the children. Vases of gerbera daisies anchored the ends of the table while plastic forks and pastel yellow napkins marched across its perimeter. The Ladies Auxiliary outdid themselves with homemade cheesecakes and a strawberry ginger ale punch.

Mrs. Simmons stood at the front of the room to give her tribute, "My favorite minister, blah, blah, blah…I remember all the times Reverend G helped us find unity during business meetings…blah, blah, blah." How could this woman be so nice one moment and send nasty letters to the elders the next? I stuffed another bite of cheesecake in my mouth and concentrated on the fresh squirt of blueberry juice.

Oh, God, help me to remember the best about Mrs. Simmons. Whatever that was. Remember the best and forgive the rest. I think I preached about forgiveness once or twice.

The children sang a little song about shining their light into the world, then Chris read the words of my favorite scripture, Psalm 46. The ancient words written by the sons of Korah and presented to the worship leader included the famous phrase, "Be still and know that I am God."

Nothing to do now, but be still and disappear into the fog.

But God, I don't want to disappear. Can I still do something for you, to serve you in some way at Cove Creek, to let everyone know that you are indeed God?

"Be still. Trust me."

Ah, there it was. That incredible voice — still with me.

Thank you, Lord. Don't leave me — ever.

The men's quartet, dressed in matching blue vests, ended the festivities with "How Great Thou Art." I finished my cheesecake and reached for another piece — with strawberries this time. Why not splurge? How often does a minister hear nice things about herself and feast on one of her favorite desserts? Even if the people, especially Mrs. Simmons, didn't exactly mean all the nice things they said, they put together a nice evening. The next time I visited the church, I would be just a regular person, forced to listen to sympathetic comments.

"Sit in the pew, Reverend G, like a good girl, and ride the old people's shuttle back to Cove Creek."

"How's the brain doing this week? We sure do miss you, but we know you're slipping."

"We're glad to have the new associate pastor who sits in your office and does your work so well. She's a bright young thing, head of her class at the seminary, experienced in officiating at communion without forgetting the words."

"Sit over here, Reverend G, with all the other old ladies and their bottle-blue hair. We'll turn up the volume on the sound system so you can hear."

Chris waved at me across the room and interrupted my

maudlin thoughts. But I was in no mood to walk in front of everyone and join him. I reached for another piece of cheesecake, knowing I wouldn't sleep with all that sugar in my cells. Blueberry topping this time. Might as well go out with a bang.

chapter 4

I n the foyer of Cove Creek, a graceful staircase spiraled upward. Staff and residents stepped on the carpet runner, fawn-colored with fuchsia roses imprinted on every other step. I loved this entrance. Every time I visited the members of my congregation at Cove Creek or prayed for the dying, the grandeur of that staircase struck me. I imagined Scarlett O'Hara in her red velvet dress as she floated down the steps to meet Rhett Butler. "As God is my witness," Scarlett said, "I'll never be..." What was it? Never be something. One of my favorite movies, and I no longer remembered that famous line. Hmm. Maybe I could rent the DVD. Now that I was officially retired, I had all the time in the world to drool over Rhett.

"How's everything going, Reverend G?" one of the staff asked me. "Getting everything moved in?"

"Yep. Doing great. Thanks." Who was that lady? She looked familiar, and obviously knew me. Tall. Dark hair. Someone I once prayed with or counseled? Hmm. Maybe it would come to me later.

My first floor apartment was down one of the offshoot wings. Jacob reserved the place, knowing I loved to be near the action of the front door and all the meeting rooms. He pegged me right — a people person even in my old age.

We carried the last of my boxes down the hallway and met Jessie who opened the door for us. The apartment, with a nice-sized living room, shone with the noonday sun. A wall of windows framed the south view, creating its own land-scape portrait. Bless Jacob for requesting this place. He knew how much I loved to watch God's creation — the birds, the plants and the monarch butterflies that migrated through Lawton Springs each autumn.

Jacob pulled a hammer from a box and nailed various frames on the wall, displaying the degrees and honors I earned throughout the years. "These ought to make you feel more comfortable, Mom. I'll put them in the same order they were in your church office."

I wasn't sure that was necessary, but if it made my boy feel better, so be it. Selah. I tried not to think about my office and all the people who once came for counseling or asked me to pray with them. Best to let that part of life go and focus on the present. Concentrate on today. Right now. Hand Jacob another frame. Try not to think about my office at the church.

A collage of international crosses anchored the perpen-dicular wall while my bookcase of commentaries stood sen-tinel on the other side. A sofa, a new recliner and a coffee table rounded out the furnishings — all coordinated by Jes-sie's outstanding sense of design.

The small kitchenette held all the amenities with its oak cabinets, a fridge and a microwave. Jessie replaced my Good-will dishes with a set of dinnerware from Pottery Barn. Nev-er in all my life had I seen such beautiful dishes with their southwestern colors of red and chestnut swirls. In fact, I rare-ly stepped into a Pottery Barn because I knew from looking at the window displays, I would covet everything inside and need to confess before sunset.

A small bath was attached to my bedroom. A twin bed came with the up-front deposit, so we dressed it with a yellow butterfly quilt — also from Pottery Barn. It was almost worth it to retire and move to Cove Creek, just to live in such luxury. For the first time in my life, my clothes hung in a walk-in closet. Too bad I owned very few hang-up clothes. Maybe Jessie would take me shopping for another pair of leather pants, especially now that Mrs. Simmons could no longer criticize me.

Jessie put away the rest of my clothes while I stared at the garden outside my spacious front window. Someone built a gazebo between a Japanese maple and a grove of hydrangeas. I planned to take my Bible out there someday and spend an hour or two in that gazebo. An hour or two with nothing to do but read my Bible. No meetings. No hospital visits. No sermons to prepare.

God, help me. I can't stand it.

Jacob and Jessie unpacked my lexicon, more Bibles and Matthew Henry commentaries. They stacked the empty boxes together and piled them on a dolly. "We'll come tomorrow, Mom, and help you with anything else you want rearranged. Love you." He pecked me on the cheek as Jessie gave a little wave.

"You have to leave so soon? You can't stay a while?"

"Sorry, no. Jess has to finish cleaning up from the last days of school, and I have some work at home. We'll see you soon."

I nodded and gave him my best fake smile. I wanted to grab his neck and hang on for dear life. Take me with you. I'm afraid. But somehow God gave me the strength to just stand there and say, "Love you."

The door shut behind them, but I hurried to open it again. I peeked around the door frame and watched my beloved children walk down the hallway, pushing the dolly together. Life had flipped upside down. This was how it felt to be in first grade and watch my mommy leave me alone with a mean teacher and twenty-one weird kids. Sheer panic and aloneness. But I was no longer in first grade with a new box of sixteen colors and a Red Chief tablet. I was Reverend G, former minister and current scared old lady.

Oh, Lord — it is not good for man to be alone...or woman...or retired minister. I cannot stay in this apartment today, no matter how beautiful my new furniture looks. I need to find other human beings, even if they are just as crazy as I. Help me, Lord.

At least I had enough cerebrum left to know that spending time all alone on my first day was a stupid choice.

Time for lunch. Jacob told me I could eat meals in the dining room or snack on something in my own kitchen. I opened my fridge, but nothing stood on its shelves — except a piece of leftover cheesecake on the second row. The cheese stands alone, I thought, laughing at my own joke. Jacob hadn't stocked the fridge yet. This seemed like the perfect opportunity to eat with the other residents. Maybe I would meet someone to minister to or find a new friend.

Earlier, Jacob took me on a tour and I remembered some of the hallways we walked. As a minister, with a focus of serving others, I once knew all the ins and outs of Cove Creek. Today, I felt like another ding-dong who couldn't remember where that stupid dining room hid. I followed the signs posted in the hallway and slowly started to recognize some of the area. Turn right after the double doors. Down another corridor. Smile at the lady in the wheelchair. Keep walking toward the delicious smell of something. Ah, there's the dining room.

Linen tablecloths of various pastels covered the small round tables. Four chairs to a table with the silverware already in place and most of the chairs filled with residents. It seemed everyone had assigned seats. Sort of like the pews that people chose in the church sanctuary. I looked out from the pulpit and always knew where Jacob and Jessie sat, as well as Chris and Mrs. Simmons. We lived in such ruts, even on Sundays. It appeared that rut-choices continued into assisted living.

I tried to sit next to a blue-haired lady, but she glared at me. "This table is reserved. My roommate and I always sit here. Together. Alone."

"Pardon me," I said and moved on. At the next table sat a man and three of those red-hat ladies. Maybe fresh from their "When-I-am-old-I-shall-wear-purple-and-red-hats meeting.

Two women chatted at another table, but when I walked toward them, I saw a set of dentures next to the water glass. A bit too nauseating for my first meal.

Okay, Lord, help me. Rejection on top of loneliness is not a pleasant way to spend the day. I guess I'm dining alone. Help me find some joy.

I walked toward a side table that faced the courtyard and pulled out the lone chair. Even though no one wanted to join me, I still enjoyed the view. Early summer flowers tried to push their faces through prenatal buds. Three sparrows and one blue-jay landed near the bird bath. I congratulated myself on still being able to count. A warm peace cuddled me.

Thank you, sweet Jesus.

During that first meal, no red gelatin greeted me, no mushy applesauce and no creamed spinach on my plate. The chef prepared a delicious chicken and rice casserole with corn on the cob and baked apples. I planned to meet this person someday and compliment him or her on the meal. The other residents ate chocolate cake, but one of the kitchen staff brought me a huge piece of cheesecake covered with blueberry sauce. Jacob must have arranged for that treat. I bit into its creaminess and missed my son all over again.

∽

That first night, sleep took a vacation. I woke up every hour and tried to figure out where I was. No familiar walls were papered with Jacob's pictures, no painted border in my bedroom that I designed myself in a fit of home decorating, no old dresser where Frank chunked out part of his head. Even though my marriage proved dreadfully sad, the setting for that sadness represented my comfort zone — my land of memories. Nothing about this apartment held memories.

I tried to kneel beside the bed, but the vinyl flooring hurt my knees. Cold. Hard.

Lord, I suppose they laid the floors in vinyl to make them easier to clean, especially when we die and leak body fluids all over the place. God, is that all I have to look forward to now? Dying and leaking?

So instead of kneeling beside the bed, I hunched up under the sheets and leaned over my pillow, sort of like a pilgrim bowing before the Wailing Wall. I thought about one of the old protection prayers I memorized years ago.

"The light of God surrounds me; the love of God enfolds me; the power of God protects me; the presence of God watches over me, and wherever I am, God is."

Yes, that was it. Hurray for me and my brain cells. I remembered the entire thing. I repeated it again, just to cement it into my mind, then over and over and over until I felt a semblance of peace recapture my soul.

Wherever I am, God is. Maybe that could be my mantra at Cove Creek. Surely God lived here. Since Immanuel lived inside me, then wherever I happened to be, Immanuel also lived. He stood beside me in the pulpit all those years. He promised to stand beside me now. Even without a particular ministry or a church pulpit, I still felt like a minister. Perhaps God sent me to Cove Creek to share his love. How many other residents lay awake tonight, wondering about their children or dreading those last moments before death? Perhaps my purpose here was to listen, to be a friend, a confidante.

Surround me with your light, oh God. Enfold me with your love. Help me to be gracious, loving and understanding with all these residents and staff people. Protect me and watch over me and let me be your minister here at Cove Creek.

∽

"So what do you think, Mom? Isn't it great?"

"Oh, my darling children. This is amazing. I am overwhelmed."

"It's called an étagère," Jessie said, as she stroked the cherry wood grain. "I found it yesterday, so we used some of the funds from the garage sale to buy it for you. See, it even has a light in the back that you can turn on. It's perfect for all your angels, and it looks great here in the corner of the living room."

"You are so right. It is perfect. Let's unpack the angels right now and put them on the little shelves."

"I'll leave you girls to do that," said Jacob, "while I go to the business office to settle things. Mom, do you want cheesecake again for lunch?"

"Absolutely. With blueberries on top or strawberries if they have them."

Jessie reached inside one of the boxes marked "Mom's angels" and lifted out a tissue bundle. She carefully unwrapped it and handed it to me. "Tell me about this one."

"Ah, the New Mexico cherub. My family visited Santa Fe every year. We rented a condo, toured all the sites and ate the most delicious foods filled with green chilies. This terra cotta angel was made from adobe. I think my father bought him for me. Let's put the New Mexico angel on the center shelf. He'll remind me of Santa Fe."

Jessie handed me a large one with a ruffled red skirt. "This one is unusual. Is it an antique?"

"Probably — an inheritance from my grandmother who made angels out of magazines. See the folds in the angel's skirt? Grandma used an old Sears catalog, then painted it red and found a doll's head at Woolworth's to top it off. She's one of my oldest angels. Probably worth something."

"Woolworth's? What's that?"

"A five and dime store that used to be downtown. Kind of like an early Walmart. We bought everything there and paid very little. They made the best cherry cola in town, and the candy counter — yum — all kinds of chocolates. I liked the malt balls. Oh, listen to me. I'm going on and on like some old lady in a nursing home."

Jessie grinned. "But I like it, and it helps me get to know you better. It's almost like every angel has a little story attached. What's the background of this one?"

She held up an AA token with paper wings glued to it. "Jacob made that angel the first Christmas his dad went to AA. Even though Frank chose to leave the program, Jacob wanted to keep this angel, to remind himself never to drink. My poor boy! He saw the very worst of his father and that awful addiction."

"He never talks about it."

"No, I'm not surprised. It was too painful — a terrible time. If only alcoholics realized what they do to their loved ones, their sweet children and even their extended families. Poor Jacob. Love him through those memories, dear Jessie. Just love him through it all."

We unwrapped more angels in silence. Crystal cherubs that shone almost with the glory of God, the special one Chris gave me after my ordination service, the blue angel I bought after Jacob was born.

Jessie kissed the Jacob angel. "Maybe I should start collecting something, to leave a heritage to our children."

I set the ordination angel on the top shelf, then turned around to face Jessie. "Children? Is this a special announcement?"

She laughed and puffed her bangs with her right hand. "No, but we're beginning to talk about it. I want to finish my master's degree, and we both want to make sure you're happy here before we make any long-range plans. We're saving the extra bedroom, just in case you change your mind and want to move in with us."

I hugged her, sniffing once again the Estee Lauder perfume. "You're a darling to even think about me, but I refuse to interrupt your lives. Now don't you put off anything on my behalf — especially the possibility of children."

Jacob interrupted our hug as he barged in with a plate of

cheesecake dollops. Tiny cupcake papers lined the various bites covered with chocolate chips, cherries and candy sprinkles. "Look what I found. We can all have one for a snack. Then you can have another big slice for lunch, Mom."

"Lunch? Did I order cheesecake for lunch?"

The smile on Jacob's face disappeared as sadness flickered in his eyes. I did it again. Forgot another moment. Stupid, stupid me.

∽

That evening, a thunking sound outside the door interrupted my Bible reading. Small intervals of thunk, thunk — then they stopped and started again. I waited until the sound faded, then peeked outside the door. A tall woman in a tweed suit moved away from me, down the hall. She carried a polished cane, one of those expensive jobs specially ordered from catalogs. That explained the thunking sound. Each time she took a step, the cane resounded on the vinyl floor.

The woman suddenly turned and saw me. "What are you looking at?" she bellowed.

Surprised at the tone of her voice, I wondered how such a terrifying sound came from such a refined-looking woman. In spite of the cane, she stood erect, seemingly confident and in total control. Chestnut-colored pumps finished off the tweed suit ensemble. One strand of pearls circled her neck. She looked as if she belonged at the top rung of the corporate ladder, not thunking her way down the hallway of assisted living.

"Please excuse me," I said. "I'm new here and still getting my bearings. Would you like to come in for a chat?"

"Absolutely not. I do not associate with people who spy

on me." And with that, she opened the door to her apartment and thunked inside. The slam of the door put an exclamation point to her exit.

Okie dokey. Just be that way. I tried to read another passage in First Peter, but that woman and her words refused to leave my mind. Maybe she hates being here. Perhaps this is her first week, just like me. Maybe she's in chronic pain. She obviously needs a cane for some reason, and she's right. I was sort of spying on her.

Lord, please help that tall woman in the tweed suit. Whatever her problem is, you know all about it. Give me an opportunity to apologize to her or befriend her. Help her to sleep well tonight, and me, too, please. Help me to somehow make a difference here at Cove Creek.

∾

The next day, I saw her again, but this time I made an even worse impression. The intercom squawked an announcement, "Everyone who wants to play bingo, come to the activity room. We're giving away lots of new prizes."

Activity room. Go meet some of the other residents. Maybe help pass out the bingo cards — a chance to be useful. But where is that activity room? Did Jacob show me around the other day? Is there a map somewhere? One of those maps like at the mall to help people find Macy's, Penney's and the food court. How can I find the activity room without a map or Jacob beside me or both?

Follow the general direction of the populace, I told myself as I opened my door. A group of residents shuffled past me while staff workers in various colors of scrubs pushed wheelchairs and directed traffic. I joined them, wondering if we looked like a group of old sheep on our way to the barnyard for the annual shearing.

Sheep. Be my shepherd, Lord. Lead me to still waters and quiet pastures where I trust you for every moment.

Down the hallway we sauntered toward a great room with a giant stone fireplace and small round tables scattered throughout. Someone obviously designed this room to be functional yet beautiful. Fabric on the chairs coordinated with vases of flowers and the artwork on the walls. The polished mantel reflected through a giant mirror with a baroque frame.

A woman in pink scrubs sat at the head table. She spun the bingo wheel in anticipation. Lopsided stacks of cards surrounded her while a gray box labeled "Bingo Prizes" took up the rest of the table space. I peeked inside the prize box and spotted some Avon bottles, several toothbrushes wrapped in plastic and assorted candy bars. The woman adjusted her name badge, and I read "Roxie: Activities Director." She must be new. I didn't remember her from my previous visits as Bible study teacher, but then, I no longer remembered the location of this room. I had to follow the rest of the sheep.

"May I help you hand out these cards, Roxie? I'm Reverend G, and I'd like to help."

"Sure, Reverend G. Glad for the assistance." She smiled.

I picked up an armful of cards and moved toward the tables. "Give me two," one woman said.

"I can handle four," bellowed a man with hearing aids in both ears.

"Just one for me," the tiny woman next to him said.

While I talked to Roxie, the tall woman with the shiny cane thunked into the room and settled herself at a back table, alone. Today she wore a lavender suit with a paisley scarf wound around her neck. Black pumps peeked under the table while her cane rested on the floor. She sipped from a glass of iced tea, and I noticed her fingers sparkled with some of the biggest diamonds I had ever seen.

Here we go, Lord. Even though I started off with the wrong impression the other day, help me to be kind to this woman. Let me be your servant today.

I moved closer to the woman and the back table, grateful I still traveled without a walker or a cane. But just as I reached her table and started to say, "Hello," my shoe wrapped itself around a chair leg and I sprawled forward. Cards flew out of my hand, sailed across the space and knocked the glass of iced tea right out of those jeweled hands.

"Now look what you've done, you oaf," she cried. "Someone get over here this instant and clean up this mess." The lavender suit already showed tea stains while the paisley scarf dripped liquid onto the suit's lapels. A lone ice cube thawed at the bottom of the over-turned tea glass. Roxie ran across the room while other staff members huffed down the hallways.

I grabbed a napkin and tried to spot clean the scarf. "I am so sorry. I didn't mean…I just tripped…let me help you."

The diamond-studded hand grabbed my wrist. "Do not touch me. Not now. Not ever."

Roxie came to the rescue with paper towels and a soothing voice. "Now Charlotte, it was an accident. I saw the whole thing. Reverend G did not mean to hurt you or ruin your clothes."

"Reverend? A woman minister? How disgusting. Everyone knows women should never be ministers and last night, she spied on me. You'd think a minister would know better."

Should I be affronted by the tone of her voice or her opinion of my vocation? Probably neither, if I wanted to share the love of God. At least I now knew the tall woman's name: Charlotte. Not that it mattered. She might never speak to me again, and I was quite sure this was the end of my bingo-helping days.

chapter 5

And then, the iced tea flew all over the place. You should have seen the anger in that poor woman's eyes." I explained the Charlotte incident to Chris, who sat in my recliner. He tilted his head back and laughed.

"Good old Tru. Helping the general public once again and proving her heart for ministry."

"Not funny, Chris. Oh, it's funny now that I think about it, but Charlotte was plenty peeved at me. She refused to come out for supper that night. Probably in her room trying to get the tea stains out of her scarf."

"I doubt that. She doesn't sound like a woman who ever does anything for herself. In her former life, she probably had servants to do all the dirty work. I wonder who she is."

"I'd like to find out, but we're not exactly on speaking terms. Other than shouting at me and inferring that women shouldn't be ministers."

"Certainly not the first time you've heard that complaint. Nor will it be the last."

"I know. I guess it no longer matters. I'm retired and not really a minister these days."

Chris leaned forward. "Now cut that out, Tru. Earning the title of minister does not necessarily mean that you stand in the pulpit every Sunday and expound on some religious treatise. It means you serve, you help others, you're available for anyone who needs anything. Your servant heart has not disappeared. You did offer to pass out the Bingo cards, right? That was helpful and that, my dear Tru, represents a type of ministry."

What was Chris talking about? "Bingo cards? I don't remember any cards. What were we talking about?"

Chris looked puzzled. He stood up and peered into the étagère. "Hey, there's that little angel I gave you. He's still holding up the little Bible after all these years."

"Yes, indeed. One of my favorite angels in the entire collection, but I think he's actually a she. Gender stereotyping, my friend. Her skirt and the long hair are a clue."

"You're saying boy angels can't have long hair? I beg to differ, besides — angels are genderless — messengers sent from God to help us." Chris reached inside the cabinet and picked up the ordination angel. "Remember how hard we studied, Tru? How determined we were to be at the top of our class?"

"I do. I was afraid I would never make it through Hebrew."

Chris replaced the angel and came over to the sofa to sit beside me. He took my hand in his and stroked it. "But we did, Tru. We made it through Hebrew and all the other classes, through all the cramming and all the finals. We made it through Frank's alcoholism and Polly's death. You'll make it through this, too. It's just another part of your journey."

Tears choked my throat. Chris always saw through my bravado to the root of the fears wrestling inside me. He patted my hand once again, then leaned over to peck me on the cheek. "Be brave, dear friend. I'll see you soon."

After Chris left, the apartment seemed incredibly empty. I decided to take a walk, so I found my Nike's in the closet and slipped on my favorite sweats and T-shirt. No one else walked the hallways, and no sounds came from the activities room. No Bingo today. No chance to make a mess of Charlotte's clothes. Oh, those were the cards Chris referred to. Bingo cards. Now I remembered. Dumb me. Dumb. Dumber. Dumbest.

I walked briskly up and down each empty hallway. One section was closed off behind large metal doors with a code box beside the door. A shiny plaque beside the door labeled it: "MC Wing". Who lived in "MC"? Maybe the really rich people, and the "MC" stood for "Mucho Cash". But then Charlotte would probably live there and that didn't make sense. She lived on the same hallway as I — with us common folks who forgot words during communion and tossed bingo cards at glasses of iced tea.

As I walked, the rhythm of my steps kept me in a prayer mode. Each step balanced the phrases as I reached out to heaven with a walking-talking poem.

Help me, God.
I want to be your servant.
Not sure how.
I've made one person mad.
Sorry, Lord.
Surely I can do something useful.
Something helpful, Lord.
Please show me how.
Let me start with Charlotte.
Help me know how.
She needs a friend.
So do I.

The afternoon sun called me outside as I walked toward a courtyard with green shrubs and fresh mulch. The area connected two wings of the building, and several plots of flowers added color. An iron bench perched in the middle of one flower bed. It seemed the perfect place to continue my prayers, but when I tried to open the door, it wouldn't budge. I pushed until sweat trickled across my upper lip and my muscles started to ache. "Why doesn't this stupid door open?"

"What's going on, Reverend G? Do you want to go outside?" Roxie appeared beside me and rubbed the small of my back.

"Yes, but I can't get this door to open."

"That's because it's coded. We don't want our residents accidently stepping outside. We need to know where everyone is — for security, you know. Let me key in the code, then when you're ready to come back in — just tap on the door. I'm working at the desk right here, so I'll hear you."

"Thanks. I won't be long. I just want to sit in the sunshine for a bit."

Roxie punched the keys on the code box, and the door slowly swung open. "Take your time. No hurry."

Did Jacob know they locked me into Cove Creek? No one told me I was a prisoner here, at least I didn't remember that conversation. When I signed the papers, no fine print at the bottom of the page said anything about the secret code. Someone needed a code to let me into the courtyard? Locked in and locked out until the staff let me back in? What kind of place was it that locked in their residents? Or maybe I should ask what type of people lived here that needed to be locked in and out.

Of course. I knew the answer to that question. I was one of those people, currently one of those questionably-lucid residents. At any moment, I might forget whether I was coming or going. Inside or outside. Crazy or sane. I needed the protection of a locked door, just in case I disappeared into another fog of memory lapse. Whether I liked it or not, this locked door represented my current reality, and I would just have to live with it. Now I really needed to sit in that peaceful courtyard, pray and breathe fresh air.

Wild daisies peeked through their spiky petals, and I bent to give them a sniff. I loved wild daisies and remembered planting some around the perimeter of my house. My house — the place where I no longer lived. The daisies I no longer watered, clipped or brought inside to put in a jar on the table. My table, where someone else now ate dinner and wondered about the old lady who once lived there.

It's not fair, God. Everything happened too fast. The retirement, the garage sale, the move. Whose idea was this, anyway? I don't remember agreeing to this arrangement.

Someone planted knock-out roses all along the north side of the courtyard. In full bloom, their red petals contrasted with the wild daisies. Good landscape idea. I remembered seeing a man mow the lawn one day. His John Deere cap perched on his head and a chambray shirt kept the sun from speckling his arms. Maybe he landscaped for Cove Creek.

Remember to find that man and thank him for this beautiful spot. Tell him how much the courtyard means to a retired minister. Is he on staff or a resident? Do they lock him in and out, too?

A wooden bench sat next to a small bush, so I sat down and studied the bush's leaves. How wonderful of God to include so many different textures and colors in His creation. Even the shades of green on the different leaves seemed unique in their design. The tiny veins God planted on each leaf, and the dark umber branches that led to the trunk of this particular shrub — all filled with a special DNA that only the Creator knew. My heart lifted in worship, and I closed my eyes to concentrate on the heavenly Artist.

Thank you, God, for designing so many beautiful plants for us to enjoy. What an awesome God you are! I'm so grateful I can enjoy this moment, smack in the middle of your beauty. Help me to remember how to focus on you, my Creator and my God.

A rustling in the bush interrupted my prayer. Puffs of Kansas breeze moved through the courtyard, but this breeze seemed more concentrated in the bush beside me. Odd. As I bent over to pull some chickweed from the base of the shrub, a white paw tapped me on the hand.

I jerked back, but the paw remained visible. It moved through the air as if searching for my hand. I eased off the bench and peered down into the bush. A multi-colored cat, waiting to pounce, hid behind one of the branches. Carefully, I untied my shoe and slipped it off. Then I wriggled the shoelaces beside the bush, hoping the cat would play. He swiped at the shoelaces, and I heard a faint purr.

"Come out here, and let me look at you. Here, kitty, kitty." I wriggled the shoelaces again. The white paw extended a little farther, and I petted it with my other hand. Another purr followed. "You don't seem to be afraid. I wish I had something to feed you."

I crouched down while the cat played with my shoelaces. In and out of his hiding place, that white paw extended — then a tiny peek-a-boo winked from his amber eyes. He seemed content to continue the game as long as I provided the shoelace.

"My thigh muscles will hurt tomorrow if I stay in this position. Okay, kitty. I'm going to stand very slowly and move toward the bench. Come on, nice kitty. Come on out, and let me pet you."

I sat back on the bench and wiggled my shoelaces. Out he came, slowly at first and then more trusting. He was a full-sized cat with multiple stripes, some yellow spots and a white face marked with a patch of brownish-gray over the nose. He crouched beside the bench, then suddenly jumped beside me and landed on my lap. After three rotations, he tucked his tail around his lower body and settled down. Like a small motor, his purr vibrated my entire lap.

"Well, I don't know what breed you are, but you're not wearing a collar. So you probably don't belong to anyone. I see a scar on your head, so you've had a fight about something. I'm glad you escaped to live another day. What shall I call you?"

I thought about Chris and our discussion about angels — sent as messengers to help us. The angel collection in my room. "How about Gabriel? Would you like to be named for an angel? Gabriel was the messenger who brought the good news to Mary that Jesus was coming soon. How do you like the name Gabriel?"

The cat continued to purr while I stroked his back. "Do they have rules about pets here? I don't remember anybody saying anything about it, but then — I don't remember everything these days. Pets are supposed to be good therapy, and you could help me. How about that Gabriel? Would you like to help me adjust to Cove Creek?"

No answer, just a flick of the tail. "Well, I'm not leaving you out here tonight. Who knows what might happen to you and surely, you need something to eat. I'll take you to my apartment and then ask Jacob about the rules for pets. At least, you'll be safe for a while."

I gathered up Gabriel in my arms and tucked him under my Jayhawks T-shirt. He snuggled close, so I crossed my arms underneath to support him. Then I rapped on the door.

Roxie appeared and keyed in the code. I turned sideways and sidled past her. "Did you have a nice time in the sunshine?" she asked.

RJ THESMAN

"Oh, yes. Thank you. See you later." Gabriel's fur tickled my belly, and I giggled. I hurried along the hallways to my apartment, opened the door and closed it quickly behind me. Gabriel slithered out of his hiding place, jumped onto the sofa and curled up against a pillow. He seemed to believe he was home.

∽

Jacob unpacked a quart of Chunky Monkey and placed it in the freezer section of my fridge. "To make up for the one that melted," he said with a grin.

"Thank you, dear one. You know how much I love ice cream. What melted and when was that?"

He settled onto the sofa with me and picked up the TV remote. "Never mind. It's not important. What should we watch? Isn't it about time for 'Wheel of Fortune'? R, S, T, L, N, E?"

"I'd rather just talk, if you don't mind. How are you doing with all these changes, Jacob? Are you getting used to the fact that I live here at Cove Creek — that I no longer live at the house or stand behind the pulpit?"

"Sure. I talked to the business office, and we'll be all right with the finances. The M&M fund helps a lot, and the rent on the house adds to your funds. Everything's going to be okay."

"You sound as if you memorized that speech, and besides — I wasn't talking about the finances. I know you'll take good care of the money. I mean how are you feeling emotionally — how are you doing in that area?"

Jacob crossed his legs and cleared his throat. "I admit the whole idea of dementia or Alzheimer's was hard to deal with at first, but Jessie and I talked about it — a lot. We're working through it together. I pray every day that you won't end up like

Grandpa, but I can't be selfish and just think about me or the changes in my life. You're the one who's going through the massive changes. Jessie helped me realize that you're the one who's grieving. This disease attacked you, Mom, and we hate it."

"Bless that girl's heart. Where is she tonight?"

"Parent-teacher conferences to close out the year and get ready for the next semester. Remember? I told you when I came in."

"Oh, that's right. You know, son, the idea of a grieving process hadn't occurred to me, but Jessie may be right. Any changes in life can bring grief, and it seems that everything happened awfully fast. I haven't really had time to process everything, but I will — in time. I'm sure everything will be all right, Sweetheart."

"As long as I can remember, you've always said that. Through everything we've gone through, Mom, you've always said, 'It will be all right.' Where do you get that positive outlook? And by the way, what is that noise in the bathroom?"

Before Jacob came, I hid Gabriel in the bathtub and shut the bathroom door. He was obviously out of the tub and scratching against the door. "What noise? I don't hear anything."

"You are such a bad liar." Jacob stood up and walked to the bathroom. He leaned against the door, listened for a minute, then opened it.

Gabriel streaked across the room, launched over the coffee table and landed on my lap. Jacob stood there with his mouth open. "A cat? You have a cat?"

"Just since this afternoon. You know, it was so beautiful outside so I went into the courtyard to pray when Gabriel made it clear he wanted to adopt me."

"Gabriel? You've already named him?"

"Don't you think his name is appropriate? An angel cat, come as a messenger to help old Reverend G adapt. Can I keep him, please?"

The reversal of roles seemed clear. I remembered a little tow-headed boy with a cowlick, who ran through the house with a small box. "I found a turtle, Mom. He's a beaut. Can I keep him? Puh-leese?"

We researched common Kansas turtles in Jacob's *World Book Encyclopedia*, found the best food at the pet store and settled Timmy the Turtle next to Jacob's bed. It was a decision I made without Frank's approval, knowing my son needed something to ease his heart. To live as the child of an alcoholic often caused adolescent depression, low self-esteem and insecurities. My son needed something to care about and respect that would not betray him. I decided to forgo the theology of submission to my husband for the mental and emotional health of my child.

Timmy lived a long life, first inside the house and then in a cage in the garage. He ate our leftover lettuce and forged a bond between turtle and boy. When he finally turned upside down and died, Jacob and I held a funeral service and buried him in the yard. We sang "Nearer my God to thee." Frank did not attend.

The grown-up Jacob shook his head. "I don't know about a cat, Mom. I'll have to check with Roxie and the director. I'm not sure pets are allowed. That's a question I never asked."

"You know, Jacob, I've never been a rebellious person. I followed the rules all my life, but I think I'm entitled now to do what I want to do — within reason. And I want this cat. I need Gabriel. Would you help me? Puh-leese?"

A grin spread across his face, and I loved him all over again. "I'll go to Pet Smart in a minute and get some litter and food. You need a scratching post, or he'll destroy your furniture. Gabriel, huh? It's a good name."

I wrapped my arms around Jacob and squeezed. "Have I told you lately that I love you? By the way, where is Jessie tonight?"

chapter 6

The next morning, I rolled over and heard a squeak. "Oh, sorry. I forgot you were in bed with me, Gabriel. My deepest apologies."

He stretched and yawned so big, I counted his teeth. Some of the back ones looked black. "You probably need a tooth cleaning at the vet. I'll ask Jacob about that, once we decide for sure you can stay."

Jacob decided to run an ad in the paper for at least a week, to see if Gabriel might have strayed from another home. Even though he wore no collar, he might belong to some little girl who cried because her beloved kitty disappeared. I certainly did not want that on my conscience, but I also wanted to be a bit selfish. I needed this cat.

We agreed on one week of stealth and talked about how to hide Gabriel from the staff until Jacob reviewed the rules about pets. Surely a week would give any former owners time to claim their pet. Determined to keep Gabriel, I also knew it might not be possible.

I'm asking for a favor, Lord. I need you to let me keep this cat. He likes me, and I like him. Since I can't be the minister I used to be and take care of my people, I need a substitute. This cat seems like the perfect solution.

I heard a baritone laugh. "Have I told you that I love you, dear child?"

I love you, too, Lord.

⤳

"Now you stay here, Gabriel, while I take my walk through the halls. I'll be right back."

Amber eyes in sleep-fogged slits peeked at me from the sofa cushion. In the middle of one of his many naps, Gabriel obviously did not care where I walked — as long as I left plenty of food and water in his bowls. After only three days with me, he had made himself at home; napping whenever he felt like it and licking my ice cream bowl after I finished a snack. At night, he curled up beside me, formed a half-parenthesis against my legs and purred until we both fell asleep. How could I possibly give him up? Jacob and I continued our hide-the-cat game and enjoyed our little secret.

I walked down the opposite hall and paused only once to say hello to Roxie at the desk. She closed a manila folder and clicked her pen. "You're looking chipper today, Reverend G."

"Thank you, Roxie. I feel great." Mainly because I'm hiding a new friend in my apartment, and I'm not going to tell you about him until I have to. I stifled a giggle behind my hand.

Up and down the hallways I marched, as I pumped my arms and huffed from the exertion. Surely my daily exercise kept me from turning into a little old curved lady, who stared at her shoes as her spine refused to straighten. Walking always felt like good therapy, as I pondered sermon ideas or prayed in step-along rhythm. Since I no longer preached sermons, I decided to practice scripture memory. So I quietly recited, "Trust in the Lord with all your heart. Do not lean on…lean on…lean on…"

Help me, Lord. I know it's not "trespasses."

"Lean on your own understanding."

There we go. *Thanks, Lord. Please don't let me lose the ability to understand the Bible. I can't stand it.*

"In all your ways acknowledge him, and he will make your paths straight." Acknowledge. What does that mean here at Cove Creek?

I acknowledge that you are still God, no matter where I am or in what state I exist. I acknowledge that you know best in every situation, even if I disagree with your methods. I acknowledge your power to keep my faith strong, even if I lose the ability to speak and no longer preach about what I believe. But please, don't let me ever stop hearing from you. I can't stand it.

One more turn and then down my own hallway. My calves began to complain as I passed Charlotte's door and headed for the end of the hall. I wondered about Charlotte's background. Who was she? A rich widow who posed as a trophy wife at all the special events around town? She didn't act like a trophy wife. Too strong-willed and not afraid to speak her mind.

Had I seen her around town or maybe read a caption under her picture in the newspaper? I was certain she was not a member of my church. Those were the people I knew best. My people. My congregation. Hmm.

Maybe she came from New York, Los Angeles or Atlantic City. Perhaps she longed for the big city life and the impressive world she left behind. Maybe she felt alone, with no place to belong — accepted because of her wealth and upbringing. Maybe her veins carried royal blood. I wanted to know her better.

Just then, Charlotte's door opened and a young woman backed out of the apartment. Her stiletto heels teetered, almost as if she lost her balance. A beautiful chartreuse suit fit her perfectly, and I felt certain she must be Charlotte's daughter. Fashionistas, both of them. I started to jog behind her, but the voice from inside the room stopped me.

"I don't care what you say, Meredith. You forced me to live in this disgusting place with all these decrepit people. I will never, ever forgive you."

"Aunt Charlotte, you are so wrong. The doctor said…"

"Humph. Deceptive physician. He was probably in on your little plan. How much did you pay him? A thousand? Ten thousand?"

"Oh, Aunt Charlotte, how can you say such a thing? Of course I didn't pay him anything. He diagnosed your illness as a moderate ischemic stroke. We even searched for a second opinion, remember?"

"Humph," sounded from inside the room.

The young woman sighed. She hoisted her coordinating bag onto her shoulder and turned toward me. I plastered myself against the wall, unable to walk past her, yet hating that I heard their private conversation.

Sorry, I mouthed the word.

She waved her hand as if to dismiss an unimportant employee. "I'm leaving now," the young woman said, "but I'll visit again. I love you, Aunt Charlotte." A slight turn on the stilettos, and she headed down the hall toward the main exit.

Close the door, Charlotte, so I can slip past you and disappear into my apartment. Let me blend into the wall or sneak away before you see me. I'm embarrassed enough already.

But the door widened, and the cane preceded Charlotte's

right leg. "Don't ever come back," she shouted as she stuck her head out the door. Then she turned and saw me. Surprise and then anger clouded her face. Her lips pursed, and I thought she might spit at me. She balanced herself with one hand on the doorknob and shook her cane. "Have you no decency? What are you doing here?"

"I'm sorry, Charlotte. I was taking a walk and ended up here. I couldn't get past without causing a scene. I didn't mean to pry…really."

"This is exactly what I told Meredith. The riffraff who live in this place that I have to tolerate — all because of some legal maneuvering against me. I wish I was dead. I wish you were dead."

Not even Mrs. Simmons wished me dead — at least not out loud. With all her emails and letters to the elder board, she never indicated that I should die. This was a first for me, and I wasn't sure what to say other than, "I'm sorry. Again, I apologize."

"Sorry doesn't cut it, Reverend. Why don't you ask your God why he lets us get so old that we're of no use to anyone." She turned around, set her cane on the vinyl floor and thunked inside. The door slammed behind her.

I stood at the end of the hallway for a moment longer, then willed my legs to move forward. Back in my apartment, I settled on the sofa and petted Gabriel. An answering purr reassured me. At least Gabriel seemed glad to see me. Fortunately, I still had enough marbles to take care of him and love him. In a tangible way, someone still needed me — even if he was just a cat.

Charlotte's comment haunted me. "No use to anyone." I understood exactly how she felt, although her world was definitely different from mine.

I struggled again with the facts. No use to anyone. No longer able to preach, to expound some incredible truth that God taught me. No more meetings to organize, no deacons to worry about, not even a pot luck to attend.

Why does God let us grow old and useless — to wither away and die in a place like Cove Creek? Although I loved this beautiful location, well-kept and with a caring atmosphere, I knew it represented my last stomping grounds. We all knew that. We lived at Cove Creek until the medical team issued the death certificate. Our next move? The Lawton Springs Cemetery.

"Life is a puzzle, Gabriel. As we age, life adds layers to our personalities and our experiences. We love someone, we marry, we have children. We buy homes and take care of them, learn a trade, work everyday, attend ballgames, go to church, learn more about trusting God.

"Then we begin to lose our loved ones: grandparents, parents and sometimes — horribly, a child. We struggle with our faith, yet somehow find the grace to keep breathing. The layers of life add wisdom that we share with friends and family. We begin to see the great cycle of history play out in our genes.

"Then dementia or Alzheimer's comes along and exfoliates us. It takes away the layers of life until we're back to adolescence or childhood. Nobody wants our wisdom, because we are no longer wise. We become babies again, unable to feed ourselves, to speak legibly or even wipe our bottoms. What is the purpose of that? Huh, Gabriel? Do you know?

He yawned.

How many times had I tried to encourage my older members with something positive? "Be a loving grandparent to your family. Pray for your children and their children. Write your memoirs and leave your family a legacy in black and white. After all, Moses was 80 years old when God sent him back to Egypt, to lead the Israelites to the Promised Land. Find a hobby for your golden years. God will show you how to live."

But what if we lose our ability to reason and no longer live as vital branches of our family trees? What if we become a joke, someone to laugh about at family reunions. "Have you heard about Reverend G? She's nutty as a pecan tree."

And if we lose our senses, how can we write those memoirs or find a hobby? How can we pray for our kids and our families if we forget how to send our heart-thoughts to God?

Moses served God at 80 and beyond, but I was only 62 and already in assisted living. Could I live here and somehow contribute for twenty more years? Maybe Charlotte was right. Maybe we should ask God to just let us die.

"Lean not on your own understanding."

This isn't my own understanding, Lord. This is reality. Cove Creek is filled with people who live in the reality of dementia or Alzheimer's or just plain old age. We're folks who have lived and loved, labored and served humanity and you; yet we are no longer needed. We're the cast-offs of society.

"I understand how it feels. They rejected me, deserted me and betrayed me."

But Lord, you never grew old. Yes, you suffered and died a terrible death, but after six hours, it was over. Your brain cells worked to the very end. You never struggled with arthritis, Sometimer's or any other chronic disease caused by living too long. Can you really understand?

"Trust me. Even though the experiences differ, I understand the emotions you feel."

I thought I was prepared, Lord. I thought my positive attitude would help me accept life at Cove Creek. I wanted to witness to the residents and staff in this place, to be an example of your love. But here I am, with no purpose and now — I'm turning into a gripey old lady.

Silence answered me as I wrestled with the age-old battle of flesh versus spirit, ego versus God. Tentacles of fear wrapped themselves around my anger and tried to choke my faith until I thought my heart might explode from the selfish warring inside. But if I ignored my Lord and his words to me, I would truly be a lonely castaway. I needed God too much to abandon whatever truth he wanted to teach me, even if I must learn that truth as an old, forgetful woman at Cove Creek. I gritted my teeth, took a deep breath and surrendered.

I love you, Lord.

He hugged my heart. "In everything, give thanks."

Okay, Lord. I know what you're saying. I cannot make sense of all this or possibly know what you want to do with me here. I do not know how to help Charlotte or anyone else when I'm losing myself, bit by little bit. Only you know why this has happened to me or why Charlotte is so angry with her niece. You are God, and you always plan for the best, for good results, because you are good. I acknowledge that you are wise, and you see the big picture. Help me to fit into that picture, somehow.

"I will direct your path."

And please help Charlotte and what was her name? Her niece?

"Meredith."

Please, Lord. Help Meredith and Charlotte to find their way back to love.

∽

"Oh, thank you, Chris. I really needed this. What a beautiful day!"

"You are most welcome. Always fun to spirit you away for a while, especially to the Plaza Art Fair, one of my favorite Lawton Springs events. How about we stroll over to Starbucks for a drink?"

Chris ordered his usual, "Just plain black, no sugar, no latté," while I chose the iced green tea. We started down the street, then Chris grabbed my arm. We dodged a kid on a bicycle who tethered his dog to the handle bars. The dog's tongue hung out of the side of his mouth as he ran alongside the bicycle.

"Great exercise," said Chris. The kid smiled.

I took another sip of my drink. "I don't know why I keep guzzling green tea. It isn't helping my brain."

"Still having those elder moments?" Chris took a sip from his cup, then grimaced. "Hot."

"Yeah. I struggle with Sometimer's, but at least I meet new people every day."

"You mean new residents are moving in?"

"No. I just don't remember them from the day before, so they're new to me."

Chris laughed. "You've said that before. You're a gem, Tru. It's great how you've adjusted. I admire your attitude."

"Don't go there, Chris. Do not compliment me. I deserve no honors of any kind. I've had a real pity party the last few days. One of the residents, Charlotte, the one who doesn't like me —she wants me to die."

"What? Why do you think that?"

"She said so, that's why. If it wasn't for Gabriel and a late night snack of Chunky Monkey, I might have wallowed in discouragement. Plus, the Lord helped me through it."

Chris stopped in front of a display of pottery. "What do you think of these? They look like your southwestern style." He turned toward me. "Who's Gabriel?"

"Hmm? Oh, that's right. You haven't met Gabriel. It's a secret, at least until I hear from Jacob. Don't tell anyone. Yes, I do like this pottery. Look at that wonderful vase over there, against the dark purple backdrop. I'll bet the artist is from Santa Fe."

As if on cue, a woman in a turquoise caftan approached us. "May I interest you in any of my work? All handcrafted, you know. Nothing manufactured in a factory."

"I love it. Are you from Santa Fe?"

"Yes. That's my home, but I use clay from the entire Sangre de Cristo area."

Chris moved past the woman. "Which is your favorite, Tru? This vase over here with the gold and turquoise glaze?" Chris pointed at the unusual vase.

"That's the one." I turned back to the artist. "How much is it, dear? I love your work."

"$550 for that one. I'm also selling a larger one for $675."

"Whew!" said Chris. "A bit steep for me."

I patted the artist on the arm. "Too much for me, too, dear, but I love your work. By the way, are you from New Mexico?"

A puzzled look shadowed her face. "Yes," she said. "Santa Fe."

Chris steered me away from the booth. "Back to the subject at hand, Tru. Who is Gabriel, other than a famous biblical angel?"

"How did you hear about Gabriel? He's a secret. Shh — don't tell anyone."

"How can I spill the beans when I don't know who this guy is."

"He's not a guy. He's a cat. My cat — at least for a couple more days and then beyond, I hope."

"I didn't know you liked cats. As I recall, you've never had a pet before."

"That's true, except for the small pets that Jacob brought home. Remember Timmy the turtle? Timmy was a great pet. Bigger animals were too much trouble — feeding them, grooming and the vet bills. I had enough trouble just taking care of Frank." Chris patted the small of my back. "Don't you see, Chris? I need this pet, this cat, for such a time as this. Gabriel gives me something alive to focus on, something to care about. Besides, I didn't really choose him. He chose me."

As we examined the sculpture display in another booth, I told Chris how I found Gabriel in the courtyard bush, how he stuck out his paw and tapped me, how Jacob and I hid Gabriel until we found out the rules about pets. Chris listened without saying a word.

I tossed my empty cup into a trash can. "So Jacob is studying all the documents from Cove Creek. Then he'll talk to Roxie and make sure it's okay to keep a cat. But I'm telling you right now, Chris, if I can't keep him, I'm going to pitch a fit. We ought to be able to enjoy something in our old age."

∞

Thursday was bingo day, so I decided to try again. But this time, I refused to pass out the cards. Act like a resident, I told myself, rather than a minister. Find a quiet table, put chips on the right squares and yell, "bingo" at the appropriate time. A

Snickers candy bar waited in the prize box — the dark chocolate kind, and I had my eye on it.

Charlotte thunked to the far table, and I decided not to speak to her. She obviously wanted to be left alone, but I smiled anyway. She glared back. Hmm. Still angry.

Please make a way, dear Lord, for me to befriend Charlotte or at least be civil to her.

I walked toward a man and woman I saw during my first week at Cove Creek. Beautiful white hair curled around her head in tiny spirals, but she gazed ahead as if not quite certain who I was or where we were. Her husband sat close by and arranged her chips. "Now darlin', you just try to put these in the right squares. I'll help you." He looked up and smiled. "You wanta' sit?"

"Thank you. I'm Reverend G."

He stuck out his right hand, gnarled with arthritis. "Bert here, and this is my beloved, Annie. She doesn't register the numbers too good anymore, but we like to try. How you be today?"

"Doing well and glad to meet you. Where are you from, Bert?"

"A little town just a stone's throw from Tulsa, Oklahoma. Claremore's the name. Famous for Will Rogers and the outdoor musical about our fine state. Our kids done moved us up here to Cove Creek when Annie had her first stroke. They live here in town and keep a close eye on us. I keep my eye on my bride." He patted Annie's hand. She did not respond.

Roxie walked over to our table. "Are you ready everyone? Bert, how is Annie today?"

"Fine as frog hair," Bert said. "We're ready to roll."

I arranged three cards in front of me and put poker chips

on the free squares. "G 63," Roxie called out. Two of my cards showed the correct number while Bert's and Annie's were empty.

"B 5."

I marked another one.

"So where you from?" asked Bert.

"O 72."

"Right here in Lawton Springs. I finished seminary in Kansas City and served at the Lawton Springs Community Church, in one capacity or another. Ministered there all my life, until just recently, when I retired and moved in here."

"N 33."

"So you like it here?" Bert moved a chip onto Annie's card. She stared at the wall.

"It's an adjustment, like anything in life, but I think I'll be okay."

"B 13."

"Sure, you will. Like I tell my Annie everyday, 'Let's be thankful for our breath and the roof over our heads.' We lived through the Depression, ya' know, and there were days, we didn't know where our next meal was comin' from. No matter how hard life gets, we can always be grateful to the good Lord for somethin.'"

"I 24."

I stared at Bert who pinpointed exactly what I needed to do. Give thanks for the good things and ignore the rest.

Thank you, Lord, for this important reminder. I need to be more thankful. Forgive me for my complaining spirit. Just because I no longer stand in the pulpit does not give me the right to gripe about my life. I'm sorry. I'll try harder to be grateful.

"N 49."

"Hey, Reverend. Lookee there." Bert pointed at the straight line of poker chips on my middle card.

"Oh. Bingo. Roxie, I have bingo."

We played three more games, but that first one was my only win. As Roxie gathered up the cards, Bert shook my hand. He moved behind Annie's wheelchair and pushed her forward.

"Come on over to our place sometime. We love company." Then he pushed Annie slowly toward the east hallway.

"Thank you, Bert. It was great to meet you. Both of you." I watched until Bert opened their door and pushed Annie inside.

Thank you, Lord, for Bert's ministry to me, for his reminder to give thanks. Gratitude is so important, and I need to remember that. You said to give thanks in everything. In everything. That includes my adjustment to Cove Creek. Help me, God, to be more grateful for all my blessings and to give thanks in everything. It was a good day, Lord, because I learned something. Plus, I now have a yummy Snickers bar.

⌒⌒

"Good news, Mom." Jacob's excited voice came through the telephone. "I looked at all the brochures and the documents they gave us when we checked in. No mention of any prohibitions against pets, and no one answered my ad in the paper about a lost cat. I even posted flyers around town with my email address, but no one responded. Then I checked at Pet Smart on their community bulletin board. Nothing there either. Gabriel doesn't seem to belong to anyone. An hour ago, I talked to Roxie and the executive director. They thought your owning a cat was a great idea, as long as Gabriel doesn't become a problem to any of the other residents. I'll pick him up sometime and take him to the vet for a checkup. We don't want him to bring in fleas or ticks. By the way, I Googled him and found out his breed. He's a tortoiseshell."

"A tortoiseshell? I've never heard of that, but how appropriate."

"Appropriate? What do you mean?"

"Well, you had Timmy the turtle. Now I have Gabriel, the tortoiseshell cat. We seem to be attracted to the same type of animal, sort of." I heard Jacob's soft chuckle and loved him all over again. "It's such wonderful news, dear boy. Thank you for helping me to keep Gabriel. I know he will behave. He seems content to just stay here with me, to eat and sleep. No reason for him to go anywhere else or bother anyone. Shall we celebrate? Can you and Jessie come over tonight?"

"We can't, Mom. I'm sorry. I'm chairman of the business meeting at church and Jessie's deep into studying for a seminar. Maybe tomorrow night. Okay?"

"Sure." I tried to hide my disappointment. "Whenever it's good for both of you. Just let me know." I hung up the phone and patted Gabriel's striped head. "Did you hear that, my friend? You get to stay forever. Good news. Just don't go wandering anywhere outside our apartment."

Thank you, God, for giving me this little friend. Thank you for working it out so that Gabriel can stay and for helping Jacob to sort through all the details. Thank you for giving me a purpose —to take care of my cat. I know he will add joy to my life here, even if all he does is sleep and eat.

But at that moment, Gabriel offered no clues about his gift or how important he would become to all of us at Cove Creek. With just a tiny warning from Gabriel or a whisper from God, I would have prayed longer.

chapter 7

iano chords of "Amazing Grace" floated from the chapel. I stopped halfway through my walk to listen. This wasn't Sunday. At least, the Sunday square on my calendar had no circle around it. No, on Sundays Jacob picked me up for church or the shuttle transported a bunch of us to the churches of our choice. I rarely walked through the hallways on Sundays, but kept that day for rest and meditation.

Yet here I was in living color, dressed in my sweats and Nike's, walking down the hall. Maybe I forgot something important that was supposed to happen today. Was it a funeral? I peeked out the front window. No hearse out there.

The hearse patrol happened regularly — about every other week. Sometimes during Bingo, sometimes in the middle of my walk, sometimes while Jacob and Jessie visited. The ambulance pulled up to the front entrance while two guys in white lab coats jumped out and wheeled a gurney inside. When the ambulance left, no lights flashed, no sirens wailed so we knew — another resident walked away with Jesus.

The chapel music changed to another hymn and now a tenor voice sang the words, "Great is thy faithfulness, Lord, unto me."

My favorite hymn. I followed the tremolo of that tenor

voice and marched toward the chapel. Sunlight filtered in through the stained-glass windows. Shafts of blue, gold and red streamed onto the oak pews. A young man sat at the grand piano and rippled through the chords, then he segued into "When the Roll is Called up Yonder, I'll be there."

Bert sat in the last row while Annie perched in her wheelchair beside him. She stared at the floor, but Bert turned around and called to me. "Reverend G. Take a load off, right here beside us."

The pianist turned toward me, and I mouthed "Great music" as I settled beside Bert. He patted my hand. "This is Annie's favorite hymn. She's really enjoyin' it."

Annie stared downward, motionless. Bert hummed the melody as more residents filtered in and settled into the pews. A familiar thunk sounded beside our pew as Charlotte made her way to the fourth row. She seated herself directly at the entrance of the pew, smoothing the straight skirt of her periwinkle blue suit beneath her. Then she angled her cane and propped it against the pew so that no one else could sit beside her.

Roxie wheeled in another resident, then hurried to the front to make the introduction. "We are so excited to have Chaplain Pete with us today. He's new to the Lawton Springs community and graciously accepted an assignment to be our chaplain. He wants to conduct Bible studies and worship services once a week. So let's all welcome Chaplain Pete."

A young chaplain, Lord, a new minister, who is now taking my place. That used to be me up there, the reverend who told Bible stories to the residents and prayed for them. My singing voice never sounded as polished as this young pup's, so I rarely sang a solo. But I loved every moment I taught in the pulpit.

Help me not to be jealous, Lord, or angry just because I've been replaced. *I knew this would happen eventually. You know the seasons of our lives, and you know this fellow — Chaplain Pete — needs to be the leader of this chapel service during this particular season of life. Help me, Lord, to be gracious. Without your help, I can't stand it.*

The residents clapped for the new chaplain as Roxie hurried back to her work. Pete stood beside the piano and said, "Let's all sing this song I've been playing. I know it's a favorite. Turn in your hymnbooks to page 252. We'll sing one verse and see how it goes."

He sat back down and played an introduction, but most of us were still trying to locate page 252. I noticed some residents who struggled to lift the heavy hymnbooks out of their wooden slots. Bert didn't seem to need the book as he joined Chaplain Pete on the first note.

"When the trumpet of the Lord shall sound…" Bert's bass blended with the chaplain's tenor while someone beside me added alto. I joined in with my broken soprano and delighted in the impromptu quartet while other residents still tried to find the correct page. Our quartet romped well into the chorus before most of the other residents started to sing.

"When the roll is called up yonder, when the roll is called up yonder…" Bert patted Annie's hand in time to the music. Her pointer finger moved slightly.

I felt my spirit lift with joy as the music entered my soul. The notes and lyrics surrounded me and helped to dispel some of my discouragement. Music soothes the soul, especially us old, forgotten souls.

"That's enough singing for now," the chaplain said as he stood and walked around the piano bench. "Let's open our Bibles to John chapter three."

Oh, sing another verse, Pete. Annie is finally responding. She needs more time with the music. So do I.

Chaplain Pete moved behind the pulpit and opened his Bible. He rattled through several sheets of paper and started to read. "John chapter three is one of the most famous passages of the Bible. In seminary, many of my New Testament classes focused on this chapter as our professors taught us about the importance of this particular exegesis. It has been reported that..."

Seminary. I wondered if Chaplain Pete attended the local seminary. Was Chris one of his professors? I would ask Chris the next time I saw him. Don't forget. Ask Chris about Chaplain Pete. I looked around for something to write myself a note. Nothing. No pencils or pads next to the hymn books. Try to remember, I coached myself. Ask Chris about this young guy.

Pete continued. "The Apostle John wrote this book and included the aforementioned passage in chapter three. You'll remember that John was a favorite of our Lord and Savior. Perhaps John sensed the importance of sharing these words so that all of us could know the Lord better."

Our Lord and Savior? Why not just call him Jesus? That's his name. Come on, Pete, you're quickly losing your audience.

I watched several heads nod as Pete droned on. One fellow on the second row laid his head on the shoulder of the woman next to him. She gave him a dirty look. Pete noticed and frowned. "But I digress," he said. "Continuing on..."

Charlotte sat as wooden and erect as a telephone pole. She seemed to understand everything the chaplain said, or at least tried to appear that way. Bert paid attention to Annie who slumped farther down in her wheelchair. I crossed my legs and noticed one shoestring untied, but when I bent down to tie it, my head bumped against the hymnbook slot. "Ouch," I said.

The alto next to me snorted. I straightened up and noticed Charlotte, who turned around to scowl at me. Chaplain Pete took out his handkerchief and wiped his forehead.

"To continue," he said. "The third chapter of John is particularly interesting as we dissect it verse by verse."

Oh, Lord. He's going to expound on each verse? We'll turn to peanut brittle by the time he finishes all thirty-six verses.

"Chapter three begins with the story of Nicodemus, who met with Jesus in the secret night hours. Nicodemus, you will recall, was an esteemed member of the Pharisees, a religious sect particularly known for its strict observance of the Mosaic law. Many of these laws are recorded in the Old Testament book of Leviticus."

God, help us. He's going to preach from Leviticus.

I squirmed in my seat. Surely Chris never taught this kid to preach like a graduate school lecture. That was not Chris's style, nor was it mine. Preach to the audience, I wanted to shout. You're losing them.

Annie fell asleep, her head nearly cradled in her lap. Bert seemed about to join her in dreamland. He jerked awake twice, then hummed quietly. The alto on my other side softly snored, her hymnbook open on her lap. It slid toward the floor. I grabbed it just before it nosedived forward.

"Sometimes," the chaplain continued, "we refer to a Pharisee as a hypocritical and judgmental person. They certainly judged our Lord and Savior with a critical viewpoint of his ministry. For example…"

Charlotte saved us. She grabbed her cane, stood up and pointed it at the chaplain. "You don't have to tell me about hypocrites. I know all about them." Then she straightened the blazer of her suit, planted her cane on the floor and thunked out of the chapel.

Other residents took Charlotte's speech as a sign to leave. They poked the people beside them or slapped shoulders to wake up their neighbors. Residents shuffled toward the doorway. Bert stood and wheeled Annie backwards. Her head snapped up at the movement, and she blinked several times. The alto beside me patted my hand and said, "Be seeing you, dearie. Maybe we can sing a duet together sometime."

I looked toward the pulpit and immediately felt sorry for Chaplain Pete. He straightened his papers and tucked them inside his Bible. A slow flush spread from his neck to his face. He moved back toward the piano and sat on the bench, but did not play. He stared at the keyboard as the chapel gradually emptied.

Roxie came in to help some of the residents move their wheelchairs. "You coming, Reverend G?" she asked.

"In a minute."

I moved slowly forward until I stood even with the first pew. "Your music sounded lovely," I said, "and you're gifted with an incredible tenor voice. Thank you for sharing that with us."

Pete looked up. I was struck by the deep brown of his eyes. He reminded me of a whipped puppy I once saw at the Humane Society.

"I struck out, didn't I? Even before that tall woman left, I lost them."

"Well, in a word, yes. But you gave it the old college try. That counts for something."

A half-grin accented his dimpled chin. "This is my first

time here, and I wanted it to be great. I hoped for an opening to witness, to lead someone to salvation. I prayed and studied for several hours and thought I was ready."

I moved closer to the grand piano and rested my arm on the lid. "Preparation is important, and I commend you for it. But always remember who you're preaching to. Who is your audience, your congregation? What level of belief do they have? What can they understand, yet what are they simply not ready for?"

He nodded. "You're the minister from Lawton Springs Community Church, aren't you? I heard someone call you Reverend G."

"Retired minister. Yes. I'm Reverend G. For many years, I served the community and preached at assisted living places, just like Cove Creek. In fact, I once stood in this very pulpit. May I give you some advice?"

"Absolutely. Anything that might help."

I noticed a wedding ring on his finger. "Do you have children?"

"Two. A girl and a boy. Five and three."

"Okay. Think about your five-year-old. The girl? Would she understand a treatise on the Pharisees or on the sacred meeting of Nicodemus and Jesus?"

"No, of course not. I'd have to simplify it for a five-year-old."

"There you go, Pete. Simplify. Some of these folks have already regressed in their mental age to that of a child, while some of us continue to move in that direction. We need simple words and easy concepts, but we do not want to be treated like dummies. These residents deserve your respect and your honor, but give the message like a brief devotion — not a lecture. Tell the story, the wonderful story of God's love. Let the Holy Spirit do the soul work while you teach the basic truth."

"Hmm. Like talking to a child. Okay. I get it. Simplify. Will you help me? Can I meet with you each week before chapel, to review my speaking topic?"

"Sure. That would be fun for me, too, but don't think of your service here as a speaking gig. Just share God's love with these folks. They need hope, a few words of encouragement and lots of music. We all love music. More of the old hymns, Pete, and less of the seminary details."

He nodded and picked up his Bible. "Can I treat you to lunch? Roxie said I was invited."

"Wonderful idea. Let's hash through a few more ideas over chicken and rice. If you play your cards right, Mr. Chaplain, I might even give you a bite of my cheesecake. By the way, do you happen to know my best friend? He's a professor at the seminary. Chris, Doctor Chris...uh Chris...oh, help us, Lord. I've forgotten his last name."

∽

Back in my apartment, I announced to the empty living room. "Gabriel, guess what? I now have a purpose. This young kid fresh out of seminary wants my help with chapel. Isn't that great?"

But no meow answered me. Hmm — must be in the bedroom.

"Gabriel, did you hear me?" I hurried into the bedroom, expecting to see those gray and orange stripes curled up on my pillow. "Gabriel."

Not on the pillow. I didn't like this game.

I peeked under the bed, then searched through the bathroom, hurried back to the living room, looked under the recliner, on top of the étagère and in the kitchen. I opened every cabinet as well as the washer and dryer. No cat anywhere. No Gabriel. How in the world had he sneaked out?

God, please, I need my cat. We've bonded. He keeps me warm at night and he's someone to talk to when I feel lonely. Don't let me lose Gabriel – on top of all the other changes in my life. Please. Help me find him.

I searched through my apartment once more, then gave up and hunted for Roxie. She sat at her desk and flipped through a catalog of colorful scrubs. One of the kitchen staff peeked over Roxie's shoulder and pointed to a blue top. "That one," she said.

"Roxie," I whispered. "I need to talk to you. It's important. In private, please."

As she stood and moved around the desk, Roxie adjusted her ponytail. Almost afraid to bring up the subject, I tiptoed beside her as we made our way back to my apartment. "I know you told my son to make sure Gabriel didn't bother anyone, but I can't find my cat anywhere. I searched all over my apartment, and I'm sure that I closed the door tightly when I left. But I cannot find Gabriel. Help me, please."

Roxie patted my shoulder. "Now, don't worry, Reverend G. He's probably just playing hide and seek with you. Cats like to sneak around and hide in funny places."

"That's what I thought, but he's not in any of his usual hiding spots. I'm so sorry, Roxie. I hate to be a problem to you."

"You're no problem, Reverend G. Don't worry about it. I'm sure we'll find him."

Again, we searched through my apartment - under the bed, in the cabinets, behind the shower curtain. No Gabriel. He was gone.

Just then, a voice came over the intercom. "Roxie, come to the front desk, please. To the front desk. Roxie."

I followed her, just in case someone had found Gabriel. Maybe the kitchen staff? How terrible! If my cat found his way to the kitchen and ate someone's tuna casserole, what would they do to him? Send Gabriel to the humane society and put him to sleep? Expel me and order me to move to some other assisted living place? I imagined Jacob's disappointment. His own mother expelled — a black mark on her assisted living grade card. What did they do with residents who refused to behave? Move us to that mysterious "MC" wing? What did "MC" stand for anyway?

Bert stood at the desk and waited for Roxie. "Well, howdy, girls. I asked for Roxie, but I see the Reverend is here, too. And how are we, this fine afternoon?"

"What's going on, Bert?" Roxie asked. "How can I help you?"

"Somethin' has happened in our apartment, and I wanted you to see it. It's the darndest thing."

Oh, no, I thought. Has something happened to Annie? But Bert seemed rather pleased about something. In fact, I noticed a twinkle in his eye.

We hurried to the apartment, as fast as arthritic Bert could walk. Good thing I still had my Nike's on. I wanted to sprint forward and find out if Annie was okay. Bert held their apartment door open.

"Ladies," he said, gallantly sweeping his arm toward Annie's bed.

She lay on top of the bedspread like a young child, decked out in her lacy nightgown. Her eyes stared upward at the ceiling, but a tiny smile brightened her face. In the crook of her left arm, all curled up with one paw over his nose slept Gabriel. His other front paw rested on Annie's right arm. He slowly opened one eye, then shut it again as if to say, "Leave us alone, please. We are quite contentedly napping."

Roxie giggled, and I joined her. Bert moved toward Annie and planted a kiss on her forehead. "My darlin' hasn't smiled for a long time," he said, and he wiped his eyes with his thumb and third finger. "I don't know whose cat this is, but I'm surely grateful. To see a smile on my Annie's face again, well, it's just wonderful."

"He's my cat, Bert. I've been looking for him ever since chapel ended. He isn't supposed to leave my apartment, but he seems to have found a good place to land."

When he heard my voice, Gabriel opened both eyes, yawned and stretched out his left paw. He settled his chin on Annie's arm and went back to sleep.

"I've got to get back to work," Roxie said. "Why don't the two of you decide how and when to take Gabriel back to Reverend G's apartment. Just don't let any of the other residents see the cat. Okay? He's supposed to be a house secret."

Bert and I nodded. As Roxie left the apartment, Bert motioned me toward a chair. Annie lay still, slowly breathing with that same smile on her face. We sat in the silence and enjoyed the quiet of the room. Gabriel slept on.

Bert watched Annie for a good ten minutes, then whispered. "We've been married fifty-seven years, and she's just as beautiful as the day we met. Even though she can't talk anymore, I know what she's thinkin'. She's picturin' a beautiful Oklahoma sunset, just west of our farm. She's gatherin' the wash off the clothesline and smellin' how fresh everythin' is from the afternoon wind. She's gonna' take that wash into the house and fold it, then make us all a fried chicken supper with all the trimmins'. She was a great cook, my Annie. She could make biscuits as light as a bobwhite's sunrise call." Bert wiped his eyes again.

Annie's eyes slowly closed as her smile began to fade. Gabriel stood and stretched his long body. The stripes along his backbone disappeared into a mass of dark gray fur. He jumped off the bed and leaped into my lap. I petted his head and smiled at the accompanying purr.

"It seems Gabriel is ready to travel. Thank you, Bert, for a lovely time with you and Annie. I'll try to keep my cat where he belongs."

"No trouble a'tall, Reverend. Me and Annie were glad to have ya'. Bring that ol' cat back any time you want."

I tucked Gabriel underneath my shirt and looked once more at Annie. She slept quietly as Bert moved toward her. He touched her cheek. "Yep. Fifty-seven wonderful years."

∽

Doc Sanders looked down my throat. "It seems you're in good health, Reverend G. You're fit as can be, and I'm glad you still exercise. Do you like it at Cove Creek?"

"It was an adjustment at first. I couldn't sleep and felt a little depressed at the loss of my ministry. I missed my people. You know, that sort of thing. But I'm getting used to it now, and I meet new people every day. Get it, Doc? New people, because I forget that I met them the day before."

He flipped through my chart and scribbled inside. "I get it. Good one. Did you know my wife is at Cove Creek? She's been there four years already."

"Sandra's at Cove Creek? I've never seen her. Wait. I think

I knew that. Didn't one of the deacons visit her on Sunday afternoons? Which apartment does she live in?"

Doc put the chart under his arm. "She's not in an apartment. She lives in the MC wing – off toward the east side."

"MC? What does that mean?"

"Memory Care. Sandra has Alzheimer's. I tried to care for her myself, but it became more difficult than I imagined, much more than I could deal with. To keep up my practice and care for my ailing wife — it was just impossible, no matter how much I loved her. Our children were all busy raising their children and working. So we called a family meeting and decided the folks at Cove Creek could do a better job than the rest of us."

"Oh, Doc. I'm so sorry. I had no idea."

He cleared his throat. "We kept it quiet, on purpose. We tried to respect Sandra's dignity and not embarrass her by telling her prognosis to everyone at church." He moved toward the door and grabbed the knob. "Now, you continue to take care of yourself. When you're ready, I'll prescribe a little something for the memory lapses. Just tell Jacob and he can call the nurse."

"Okay, Doc. I will, but not yet. I'm not ready to travel down that take-your-medicine-every-day trail. I still think for myself, at least most of the time. But I meet new people every day. Get it? It's a joke."

He nodded and left the room. Jokes had never been my specialty.

∽

We finished our ice cream, and Jessie took the bowls to the sink. Jacob stretched out his legs and pulled the lever on the recliner. "Good ice cream, Mom. I'm stuffed."

"Me, too. There's nothing quite like Chunky Monkey, unless it's cheesecake with blueberry topping. Somebody should invent that flavor of ice cream — cheesecake with blueberries. I'd buy the first gallon."

Jessie washed out the bowls, dried them and put them in my cabinet. She seemed unusually quiet this evening, and I wondered what was wrong. Tough day planning for the new school year? Worried about her students? Maybe she didn't feel well. Too much ice cream?

I hated to meddle, but then again, I hated to sit around all evening and try to converse with my loved ones if something was wrong. Maybe I could help. Old Reverend G used to be a trained counselor and all those years of experience counted for something. Of course, experts always said, "Never counsel your own family members." But if my daughter-in-love needed help, to heck with the rules.

Help Jessie, Lord, whatever the problem. Help us all.

After Jessie settled herself on the sofa, she grabbed a pillow and clutched it to her chest. A classic sign of stress. Hang on to an inanimate object and try to find security. Double your fists as you hang on to the pillow — sign number two. Jacob crossed his arms in front of his chest. Sign number three. If somebody didn't tell me the truth pretty soon, I was going to blurt out the question, "What's troubling you?"

Jessie sighed deeply. Sign number four. "Jacob," she said. "Are you going to start?"

Bless you, my child. Get it out in the open. Whatever it is, we can deal with it if we know what it is. The truth shall make you free. Help us, Lord.

Jacob leaned forward and popped the recliner into the

chair position. "Mom, we need to talk about something that Jessie and I are going through."

I took a deep breath. *Not cancer, dear Lord, or some other terrible illness. Not my beloved children with health issues. Please. I can't stand it.*

Jacob cleared his throat. "I've been seeing Doc Sanders for a while and he suggested a counselor — to help deal with my problems. Jessie suggested it first, but I was stubborn and refused to listen. She recognized the problem and wanted me to get help."

My heart flipped with a mommy-leap, suddenly afraid for my son. I grabbed my own sofa pillow and clutched it tightly. "Go on, dear boy. I'm listening."

"Doc prescribed some anti-depressants for me, and they seem to help. But he also suggested I get to the root of the problem so that I don't always depend on some kind of medicine. He believes in finding the solution, you know."

"Yes, wise advice. Doc is wonderful. So you've seen a counselor?"

"Uh-huh. She works in the same strip mall where Doc has his office. Jessie and I met with her together — twice — and I schedule appointments once a week. I think we're making progress, don't you, Jess?"

She turned toward me, and I saw fresh tears hanging off her eyelashes. I reached for the Kleenex box on the coffee table. Jessie dabbed at her face, then grabbed the pillow again. She answered in a husky voice, "It's kind of like peeling an onion, layer by layer. Each time we meet with the counselor, then talk about it together, we peel another layer and feel the pain. But the counselor says we have to feel it to heal it. I like that phrase."

"So true," I said. "Can you tell me about the root of the

problem?" *Please don't say it's my fault. Dear God, please do not let me be a stumbling block to Jacob and Jessie.*

"It's all wrapped up in what happened to you and especially...what happened to Dad."

Oh, God, it is me. I can't stand it.

"What have I done, Jacob? Please forgive me, whatever it is."

He jumped out of the chair and fell on his knees beside the sofa. As he took my hands in his, he kissed my ring finger. The empty finger. "No, Mom. It's not your fault. Please don't feel guilty. It's just that when Doc diagnosed this uh, problem you have, it resurfaced the feelings that I buried about Dad, about his drinking. I suddenly felt like an orphan, like both parents were taken from me, and I was mad at God, mad at the world, even mad at Jessie — for no reason."

Now I needed the Kleenex. I took one and handed the box back to Jessie who wept all over the pillow. I wiped my eyes and patted Jacob's face. "That's why we searched for help when you were a teenager. Remember? Alateen for you and Al-Anon for me. I thought the meetings were helpful. I thought we survived your dad's addiction rather well. Remember the Serenity Prayer?"

We stated it together. "God grant me the serenity to accept the things I cannot change, the courage to change the things I can, and the wisdom to know the difference."

We smiled at each other, and I rubbed Jacob's cowlick down.

Oh, God, I tried. I did everything I knew to save my boy from the ravages of his father's addiction. Blast you, Frank. You hurt our son.

"Alateen did help, Mom, and I still read through the materials. But somewhere down deep, I felt resentment toward Dad and transferred that to God and then to Jessie. All those times Dad promised to come to my baseball games, then we found him passed out on the kitchen floor. Or my band concert when I played the trumpet solo. Dad double-dog promised me he would be there, remember? Chris found him at the bar and brought him home, long after the concert was over."

"I know, Babe. I'm so sorry. Such an awful time, the way your dad hurt you, how he mistreated us both. I hated it."

Jacob looked at me and squeezed my hand. "I know it wasn't your fault, but I wonder why you stayed with him. Why clean him up again and again? To protect me? Why not just divorce him and start all over with someone else?"

I took a moment to think back, to collect memories of that terrible time. "It isn't easy to explain, Sweetheart. I guess I always believed your father might change. I prayed for him, hoped for his decision to pursue sobriety. And, of course, a divorce would have eliminated my job. Back then, churches never hired divorced ministers. That meant poverty, losing the house and moving away from your friends until I trained in another field or found a different job. I guess the horror of those moments seemed more comfortable than the insecurities of the unknown. I'm sorry, Jacob. Please forgive me."

Jacob nodded. "Please don't feel guilty. I'm beginning to understand. It's odd that the anger spews out now — all these years later — and it affects our marriage. We're working really hard not to let it destroy us, especially now."

"Especially now? What do you mean? What else is going on?"

Jessie scooted over on the sofa and put her arm around my shoulder. "We've decided to start our family. If we get pregnant in September, I can teach through this next school year. Then if our baby comes in June, I'll have the summer to recuperate. But we want our marriage strong and healed before we make a baby."

I stroked her cheek. "You are so wise, dear ones. Babies are a major blessing and a disruption at the same time. You need a healthy marriage, and I am so proud of you for working things out."

Thank you, God. They want to give me a grandchild. They're working on their marriage. I am blessed.

"Well, the counselor thinks we have a good chance for complete resolution," said Jacob. "She's encouraged by our progress over the last few weeks. And the fact that we have a timeline keeps us motivated. Besides, we want our baby to know you before…"

Jacob looked over at Jessie with that sad expression that I saw every time Frank stumbled around the house. Sadness, regret, inner turmoil. I hated Frank for making my boy sad. I hated how he wounded our son, then and now. I hated how alcoholism destroyed families, but knew I needed to take action and proactively come against my hatred.

I choose to forgive, Lord. Help me to forgive not only Frank and his unwillingness to leave his addiction, but also to forgive myself. I denied my son's pain in the midst of my own horror. Help me to forgive you as well, God. For some reason, you allowed this ugly monster into our lives. I don't understand, but I choose to forgive. The question is why, but the answer is Who. The answer lies with you, God.

"What do you mean, dear ones?" I asked. "You want a baby before…before what?"

Jessie looked down and studied the wadded up Kleenex in her hands. Jacob cleared his throat, and suddenly, I knew. They wanted my grandchild to know his grandmother before

I disappeared into the ashes of Alzheimer's. They wanted me to hold their child before I was too feeble to care for such a tiny babe. They wanted me to share their joy before I could no longer smile, pray or think clearly. They wanted good memories for the scrapbooks in their souls.

I reached on the coffee table for my Bible and turned to Psalm 91. Clearing the pain from my throat, I read, "He who dwells in the shelter of the Most High will abide in the shadow of the Almighty. I will say to the Lord, 'My refuge and my fortress, my God, in whom I trust.'

"Abide and trust — two action words we focus on, my darlings, no matter what happens. In this case, abide means to rest. As you talk to the counselor, abide in the Lord, rest in him and trust in each other. As you move toward becoming parents, rest in God's timing and trust that he knows what is best for you. And I will do the same, rest and trust that God will somehow keep me sane so that I can enjoy this blessed child. Let's all just abide and trust."

chapter 8

Early Sunday morning, a knock sounded on my door. Who in the world? Too early for the church shuttle, and certainly not Jacob. He never visited before the sun peeked in my windows. Had Chris promised to come by and I forgot? Hmm. Nothing written on my Don't Forget Pad by the phone.

Oh, Lord, I have a bad feeling about this.

Roxie stood in the hallway. "You need to come with me," she said in a serious tone.

"What's wrong? Have I missed a meeting or forgotten to sign an important piece of paper?"

Roxie said nothing, but walked just ahead of me down the east hallway, toward Bert's and Annie's apartment. She opened the door and ushered me in. There sat Gabriel, curled up beside Annie, his left paw on her hand.

"Oh, no, how did this happen again? Gabriel, you're a naughty cat. I'm so sorry, Roxie. It won't happen again...Bert?"

Bert sat beside Annie's bed, his head resting beside hers on the pillow. Annie stared upward, the same as always but this time – her features completely calm. She lay still, too still, and I saw that her chest no longer moved up and down. Annie's spirit had left her stroke-ravaged body, and she no longer struggled with the injustices of life.

Roxie gripped my hand. "It just now happened. Bert hit the call button, and I came running. The first thing I saw was Gabriel, just like that — his paw on Annie's hand. Isn't that something?"

"Yes. Beautiful and horrible at the same time. We never get used to the finality of death, but sometimes we deny the beauty of it. Just look at Annie's beauty now. You can tell by the look on her face — her soul is at peace and in a better place."

Bert moaned, a guttural cry of deep pain. "Oh, my Annie. I wanted to go first. I can't live without you. Why didn't God let me go first?"

Roxie moved toward Bert and put her hand on his shoulder. "I'll call your children, Bert. They need to know so they can be with you, help you with the arrangements. Reverend G? Would you stay with Bert for a moment?"

"If he wants me to. Certainly, I'll stay." I settled in the recliner as Roxie left the room. I knew Bert needed his space, to say his own goodbyes and deal with the first moments of grief. I wanted to be present, yet not intrude.

Give me wisdom, Lord, and please comfort Bert. Be with the children as well — with all of Annie's friends and family. Thank you for the years you gave her on earth and for their lovely marriage. Send comfort, Lord. Send peace.

Gabriel jumped off the bed and leaped onto my lap. He circled twice, then tucked his tail under him and sat down. His purr vibrated my legs, and I patted him between the ears. "Good kitty. You stayed with Annie while she traveled Home, didn't you? You helped comfort her on the journey."

As I looked around the apartment, a number of family portraits seemed to echo the happy family life of Bert and Annie. The parents with their young children — Bert with black hair and Annie glowing with a beautiful vitality. Graduation photos with various colors of gowns and mortarboard tassels, baby pictures — some blue, several pink. More family pictures surrounded the largest frame in the middle — the wedding picture of Bert and Annie that started this family tree.

Thank you, God, for all the decades of joy you gave Bert and Annie. What a wonderful blessing to love and receive love for a lifetime. Thank you for all these children and grandchildren — for the legacy you created for this family.

I sat quietly and stroked my cat as Bert cried and occasionally touched Annie's face. I started to hum, "When the Roll is Called Up Yonder," remembering how recently we sang that hymn. Death always comes as a surprise, even for people in hospice, even when we expect a terminally ill patient to expire. No matter how advanced the science of dying becomes, the moment when life ceases is never a given until it actually happens and the medical team records the time of death. Then we all remember how fragile and mortal we are — how quickly and unexpectedly life ends. Yet if we're not ready to accept death, then we rarely know how to embrace life.

Now holding Annie's hand, Bert hummed along with me. Then he stood beside her and haltingly sang the words she loved, "When the roll is called up yonder I'll be there." His voice cracked, but with each verse grew stronger as his faith overshadowed the pain. During the last verse, Bert belted out the words with powerful force, singing full fortissimo through the final stanza. With tears streaming down his face, he worshipped the God who had taken his beloved wife away. In spite of the loss, his face radiated with joy and the three of us — a grief-stricken husband, a retired minister and a tortoiseshell cat shared in the glory of eternity.

∽

Chaplain Pete sat in my recliner as Gabriel and I cozied up on the sofa. "I need some ideas for this week's Bible study," he said, flipping open his yellow legal pad. "What do you think? A topical study? Or what about a video on the Holy Land? I toured the Middle East several years ago, and that area is always in the news. Do you think they would like that?"

I frowned. "No, not really. Someone else's trip usually fails to inspire, don't you agree? Have you ever felt trapped in a friend's home, forced to watch his summer vacation movies? Boring. None of us residents go anywhere unless someone picks us up for an outing or the shuttle comes for an activity. We miss our freedom and someone's tour of the Holy Land only reminds us of that loss. So a video about the Middle East probably won't fly."

"What then? A topical study? We're into the summer months. How about freedom in Christ for the Fourth of July weekend?"

"Remember, Pete. Simplify. You're not here to expound. Encourage the residents and possibly, entertain them a little bit. You have probably ten minutes before some of us start nodding off. That's not your fault. It's the medications, the warmth of the chapel and the inactivity of our brains."

Gabriel stretched and walked across my lap to the other side of the sofa. I looked across the room toward my bookcase and the reference books alphabetically stacked. "How about one of the characters in the Bible? The Old Testament includes so many great characters and interesting stories. Everybody likes to hear stories."

"Great idea. What's your favorite book in the Old Testament?"

I thought a moment. "Actually, I like all thirty-nine. How about that, Pete? I remembered the Old Testament has 39 books, and the new has 27 for a total of 66. Wow, a good math day. Anyway, each book includes so much truth about God's love. The Bible is basically God's love story to mankind."

An inside smile lit up my soul. 66 books. How about that? Pete raised his eyebrows. Ah, yes, he needed an idea. "How about Genesis? The stories in the book of Genesis always interest me, because they tell us how everything began. Start with Adam. Then do something on Eve. Just one character at a time. Keep it short. Keep it simple, but don't treat us like we're idiots. Just tell the story."

Pete smiled. "That's a great idea. Maybe I'll compose a little song about Genesis — something about the beginning of mankind or the days of creation. I remember you told me the residents like to sing."

"Right. But again, simple. Okay?"

"Okay. Thanks. May I pray for you, Reverend G?"

"Of course. Gabriel and I always welcome prayer." It was a sweet petition, as the chaplain asked God to take care of us, keep us safe and mindful of God's love. Surely God hovered with joy over this young man and his pure heart, a chaplain who just wanted to serve the residents of Cove Creek.

"Amen," said Pete.

"Amen and thank you. Now, did we decide what you're going to talk about in chapel this week?"

Pete looked a little puzzled. "Genesis, remember? One of the characters or maybe the days of creation. I need to leave now. Thanks for your help." Pete closed the door behind him, and I turned toward Gabriel.

"I did it again, Cat. I forgot what Pete and I talked

about. Maybe I should talk to Doc Sanders about those new medicines."

Gabriel yawned and put his paw over his nose.

∽

Chris arranged a blanket on the grass beside Conway Lake. All around us couples and families laughed together, picnicked and waited for the fireworks to begin. I passed Chris the sack from Kentucky Fried Chicken and heard my stomach rumble. I could already taste those baked beans, crispy chicken strips and the coleslaw I ordered.

"What a great idea, Chris, to come out here for the Fourth. I was so disappointed when Jacob said they were going over to Jessie's parents to celebrate. Thank you for rescuing me from my gloom."

"Hey, I'm selfish. I hated to stay home and watch fireworks on the boob tube. Besides, I was hungry for wings."

We munched in silence, enjoying each other's company and the presence of young families all around us. I felt as if a fresh breeze blew through my soul as I watched the children play on the swings and the teeter-totters. One red-headed boy threw sand at his sister and laughed as she squealed, "Mommy. Brad's getting me dirty. Make him stop."

The sun started to disappear, leaving an orange trail along the horizon. Mothers sprayed insect repellent on their children. Chris packed up our trash. "So you're feeling better, you said? Like you have more of a purpose now?"

"Uh-huh. Chaplain Pete visits me every week, and we review what he's planned for chapel. He's made a lot of progress, simplified the stories, added more music, you know. I think the residents enjoy the character studies, and we sing more verses to each of the songs. Pete is getting the hang of it. He has such a good heart."

"So who did you study this week?"

I thought for a minute. "I don't know. Somebody from the Old Testament, from Genesis, I think. I'm sure it was a good story."

Chris struggled to his knees and groaned. "A little help, Tru. I'm trying to stand up, but the old bones won't cooperate."

I hopped up and gave him my hand, but one tug from Chris and I fell flat on the blanket. We both laughed. Chris reached around my waist and pulled me close. "You are the funniest little lady I've ever known."

His breath touched my cheek, and I smelled his aftershave. He stopped laughing and a serious, yet surprised look passed over his face. My heart flumped, and I wondered if this was how it felt to have a cardiac episode. What else could this lovely yet scary feeling be? Gas from the cole slaw? Too much fresh air? Unless it was…no, it couldn't be. But why not?

Well, God, what am I supposed to do now? I think I'm falling for my best friend.

Some kid threw a ball onto our blanket. Chris and I both jumped. The kid ran across my legs, reached for the ball and said, "Sorry."

Chris cleared his throat, rolled off the blanket and managed to get to his feet. I focused on his shoes, black flip-flops. Neither of us spoke for several minutes.

"I know what we need," Chris finally said. "Ice cream. I'll take our trash to the bin over there and come back with some ice cream. Vanilla okay?"

I found my voice, but it cracked. "Strawberry, if they have

it. Probably don't have Chunky Monkey."

Chris flip-flopped away just as the first fireworks popped golden diamonds into the sky.

∽

During one of my daily walks, I noticed Charlotte's niece alone in the courtyard. Her perfectly highlighted hairdo seemed out of place against the despair on her face. Sadness pasted itself onto her smooth complexion. I tapped on the glass door and motioned to come outside. "Okay?" I mouthed.

Meredith nodded and patted the bench beside her. No smile yet. Maybe I could help.

"Roxie, would you please open the door? I need to spend some time outside with Charlotte's niece."

The door slowly opened, and I walked outside. "Should have brought my sunglasses or my tanning lotion," I said, trying to make light conversation. "Bright sunshine today."

Meredith only nodded and clasped her hands together, but in the movement, I saw the family resemblance. The fair skin, the carefully manicured nails, the almost royal posture. These were refined women, Meredith and her aunt Charlotte. Probably wealthy and successful — but oh, so sad.

I sat beside her, aware of my old sweats with a hole in one knee. Never one to pay attention to fashion for myself, even Goodwill rejected most of my clothes. But I always seemed to notice the clothes of others, especially when I counseled wealthy families or now, as I tried to find common ground with Meredith.

Help me, Lord, to be a friend to this young woman. Give me an opening to talk to her and help me be a good listener. She's obviously distraught about something.

We sat in silence for several moments. A slight breeze cooled the afternoon humidity. I looked at the bush where I discovered Gabriel and smiled. The story of Gabriel seemed like a good place to start.

"Did you know I have a cat?" I asked. "It's supposed to be a secret, and I keep him hidden in my apartment. His name is Gabriel, named for the angel, you know."

Meredith stared at me. "I hate cats."

"Oh." Wrong topic. "Are you allergic?"

"No. I just hate the way they sneak around and jump on things and surprise people. Aunt Charlotte hates dogs, but I don't know what she thinks about cats. My husband, Paul, hates all kinds of animals."

"Oh, you're married. Do you have children?" A gigantic yellow diamond on her left hand sparkled in the sunshine. How many carats? Jacob probably knew all about diamonds and how to calculate the price for each setting. Remember: tell Jacob about the ring. Don't forget. The giant diamond ring. Stop it. Focus on Charlotte's niece.

Meredith shook her head. "No. We have no children. Paul never wanted any, and truthfully, I was never certain I could be a good mother. It's kind of in the family genes. Women in my family make great business partners, but we are not domestic. My mother spent most of her time at work, then signed me on as an intern as soon as it was legal." She crossed her legs, the snakeskin pumps a perfect coordinate for her white satin skirt. "What about you? Aunt Charlotte told me you were a minister, but are you married? Children?"

"I have one son, an amazing young man named Jacob. I was widowed rather early in life. My husband was only forty-two when he died."

"Oh. That's terrible. I'm so sorry. Was it a car accident?"

"Yes, in fact, a tragic accident. Frank was killed by a drunk driver." I failed to mention, on purpose, that Frank was his own drunk driver. He wrapped our car around a tree, created his own metal coffin and ended the tragedy of his life. Throughout the years when people asked me how my husband died, it always seemed easier to say, "He was killed by a drunk driver" than "Sauced out of his mind, he drove into a tree."

I remembered how I felt when the police knocked on my door and told me what happened. Weary from a lifetime of grief with Frank, I could not force any tears. Not then nor later when I held my son and told him Daddy would never come home. No tears puddled down my cheeks when I saw Frank at the funeral home, decked out in his best suit and finally at peace. I only felt relief. The accident claimed no other lives. Frank sent only himself to the morgue.

For the millionth time, I wished Frank had been strong enough to stay sober. Maybe I should have done more to help him, prayed harder, tried to be a better wife. Ever since the day I discovered him drunk in our basement, I wondered how to thwart his addiction. Beg him to stay away from it or fast and pray more diligently for his healing? Sometimes I wished for the gift of discernment, to speak convicting words to my husband or come up with a magic formula to cure his addiction. But what good would discernment do any of us now?

Forgive me, God, for my bitterness toward Frank. After all these years, I'm still mad at him and mad at myself. Help me to remember that we all make mistakes. None of us is perfect, and you love broken people. That's why we need your grace.

Meredith continued. "Aunt Charlotte divorced Uncle Lee after two years. They never had children. Her child was the company she founded. Did you know she was CEO of the largest tech support company in Kansas City? We went global before any of the competition. Aunt Charlotte is my hero, and now she's so angry with me. You may not believe this, but we used to be very close — almost like best friends. We worked so well together. I was COO. We both loved the work, and we grew our team, before she retired and moved in here. She hates me now, because I hold her position at the company. I now sit in her chair."

"Oh, Honey, I'm sure she doesn't hate you. Her anger and frustration just come out when you happen to be here. She doesn't have anyone else to target — except me when I spill her iced tea."

Meredith snickered. "She told me about that. You threw the bingo cards at her."

"Not on purpose. I tripped and they flew out of my hands. Not one of my better moments." I reached down and picked a chickweed from the ground. Then I twirled its tiny purple flowers around, wishing for some wisdom to share — some way to help this young woman.

"You know, Meredith, relationships are always a little tricky, especially when one of the persons seems so unhappy. Maybe your Aunt Charlotte feels out of place. Not many of us were as successful in life as she was. It must be terribly difficult for her to be out of the mainstream of society."

She nodded, so I plunged ahead. "I know how difficult it was for me to retire. I suddenly felt useless, without purpose, after a lifetime of helping others. My forgetful moments came more regularly, and I was scared. We call it Sometimer's." I nudged Meredith with my elbow, but she did not laugh — not even a smile.

"Yes, I see so much anger in Aunt Charlotte. She gets furious when she forgets something."

"Maybe it's not anger you're seeing, but fear."

"Hmm. Fear. I never thought of that. Her stroke caused some paralysis, but she conquered most of it through physical rehab. Maybe she's afraid of another stroke or a complete mental breakdown. But what can I do to help? Every time I come to see her, she attacks me about taking over the company. She resents that I now sit in her office and run the company she propelled forward."

Help, Lord. What can we do for Charlotte? You know what she needs. What would I want if I were in Charlotte's place?

I twirled the chickweed until it started to leak brown sap on my fingers. Meredith grabbed it from me and tossed it behind her. Another take-charge woman, just like her aunt.

"You know, dear, I'm not a businesswoman by any means, but I always feel better when people ask me how to do something related to ministry. Maybe if you ask your aunt for advice, bring some of your papers and go over them with her, help her feel as if she still contributes."

For the first time that afternoon, Meredith smiled. She patted my hand. Her diamond glittered. "Make her feel like she still contributes to the company. That's a great idea, Reverend G. I think I'll try it. Thank you."

"Well, good luck. Remember God loves you, dear. And he loves your Aunt Charlotte. He'll help you through this. He always loves to help his children."

∽

Roxie nudged me as I stepped back into the building. "It happened again. Come with me, please."

I followed her to the doorway of the MC unit and watched as she coded in the numbers on the keypad. We entered a hallway similar to all the others at Cove Creek, except nurses and other medical people in white coats walked briskly through doorways, typed at the computer stations or carried trays of medicines. This was clearly a different setting, and I did not like it.

Please, God. Don't let me end up here. This is more like a hospital for those who can't help themselves any more. This does not look or even smell like the Cove Creek I know. I can't stand it.

At the second doorway on the right, Roxie ushered me into a room. In the center of the floor stood a hospital bed with beeping monitors on either side. A mobile tray with an assortment of helpful things stood beside the bed — an empty bedpan, a glass with a crooked straw plopped in it and a small packet of Kleenex. In the center of the bed, so small I barely saw her, lay a white woman — her skin the same color as her hair and the albino sheets. Her head moved from side to side in a rhythmic dance, perhaps from some troubling memory in her past. She muttered, "Not now, not now" over and over. Curled up beside her with his paw on her right hand, lay my wandering cat.

"Oh, Gabriel. Not again. Bad kitty. What am I going to do with you? I'm so sorry, Roxie. I have no idea how he's getting out."

"Well, obviously, we have to find a way to keep him in your apartment. I do not want to take him away from you, Reverend G, and he's really not creating a problem. I'm just worried about some family member who might see a cat in their loved one's room and get upset. We have to consider public relations, you know, and there's always the possibility of some lawyer suing us for endangering our residents. Liability issues are everywhere in assisted living."

"Of course," I said as I picked up Gabriel and hid him under my T-shirt. "I'll take him back home right now."

"Not yet. Maybe you could pray for Marie here. She's so agitated today, and we don't know why."

"Of course, I'll pray. Bless her heart." I handed Gabriel to Roxie who bowed her head over his striped ears as I prayed.

"Dear God, please help Marie today. She's upset about something and only you know what that is." I patted Marie's hand and held her fragile fingers. "Please give peace to this woman, dear Father. Help her to rest well. Let her know that she hides in the shadow of your wings, that you are with her right now — in this room. Give her peace. In the name of your son, Jesus...amen."

"Amen," echoed Roxie. She handed Gabriel back to me, then pressed the call button. The nurse at the station answered and Roxie said, "We're leaving now. You might want to check on Marie in a few minutes."

Roxie opened the door for me, then turned back and looked at Marie. "She's a dear soul, and we...wait a minute... look. Reverend G, look."

I turned around and saw that Marie no longer wobbled her head back and forth. No words came repeatedly from her lips. She slept quietly, a look of contentment on her face.

"Thank you, Lord," I said as I hugged Gabriel.

"Yes, indeed," said Roxie.

chapter 9

ert sat by himself, three bingo cards spread out before him. His head sagged forward, but when I pulled out the chair across from him, he raised his head and tried to smile.

"How's it going, Bert?"

"Well, I can safely say I've had better days. You see, this woulda' been our fifty-eighth anniversary. I was so hopin' my Annie and me would make it to sixty."

"Fifty-seven years of marriage is quite a record in today's world."

"Yeah, but fifty-eight woulda' been a comfort and sixty woulda' been a blessin'." He swiped his sleeve across his nose and sniffed. "I miss her so much, Reverend. Even though I know she's with Jesus, I miss my Annie so much."

"I'm sorry, Bert. I wish I could help."

"Thanks. They say it just takes time. Guess that's all I've got now. Time."

I arranged two bingo cards in front of me and waited for Roxie to call out the first number. At her usual table in the back of the room, Charlotte sat alone. She glanced toward me, and I waved. A scowl planted itself on her face.

"G 62."

I marked my free spaces, found G 62, then glanced at Bert.

What can I say, Lord? This man obviously needs to grieve, and I don't want to offer him any platitudes. How can I encourage him? Grief is so hard, Lord. You know that. You carried all our sorrows and you understand all our griefs, including Bert's loss of his beloved.

"B 5."

Bert and I both moved poker chips onto one of our cards. I tried to find a lighter subject. "What did you do for a living, Bert? What was your occupation?"

"N 43."

"I was a farmer. Annie n' me owned two sections plus another quarter of land, and we raised wheat. Kep' a few cattle. Butchered every year n' worked hard every harvest. It was the best place to raise our young uns. I shore do miss the farm life."

"O 72."

"Annie was a school teacher, for the little uns. She taught 'em their ABC's and 1-2-3's. That way, she was home with our kids after three o'clock every day, an' she was home in the summers t' help with harvest. My Annie was the best cook. Fried chicken n' pork chops that'd charm the chest hair off anyone. Men used to line up t' be my farm hands just so they could eat Annie's food."

"N 44."

"Yessir, and gardenin'. Annie kept a big garden n' put our kids to work pullin' weeds. We always ate fresh stuff from Annie's garden: green beans, tomatoes, taters, onions n' such. Then she canned 'em, so we ate off her garden all winter long. Nobody went hungry at Annie's table, no sir."

"B 7."

We sat quietly for a while, marking our cards. One of the

kitchen assistants passed out lemonade and vanilla pudding with graham crackers on it. Bert took a big bite. I ignored mine, wishing I had cheesecake.

"O 76."

Just as I marked my card, I thought of an idea. "You know, Bert, I sat outside in the courtyard the other day and noticed lots of chickweeds. Maybe you could go out there sometime and do some weeding. You'd have to ask Roxie, of course, and maybe the landscape guy — the one that wears the John Deere cap."

"N 37."

"Maybe so, Reverend. Yep, that's an idea. Gimme somethin' to do with these long days. Takin' care of the ground is what I do best. Both Annie 'n me respected the land."

"B 13."

Bert moved another chip to the B column. "Hey, Reverend. Maybe I could till a little garden out there and plant some things in honor of my Annie. A tomato bush or even a coupla' flower plants. Annie liked those mary-golds. Said they was good for keepin' bugs away. Might even help my Arthur-itis to dig in a garden. Get it? Arthur-itis."

"I 22."

I laughed with my friend across the table. "A garden for Annie. That's a great idea, Bert. Go for it."

Thank you, Lord. Thank you for giving Bert something else to focus on besides Annie's death. Thank you for directing this conversation. Please help this gardening idea to happen. Bert needs it, Lord.

"N 35."

With hope shining in his eyes, Bert looked up from his card and smiled. Then he stood up and hollered, "Bingo."

On my daily walk, I noticed a lady who sat alone in the front lobby. The wingback chair, covered in gold and brown tapestry, almost swallowed her. She reminded me of the tiny Alice in Wonderland pictures, the little girl plopped in the middle of a giant chair.

Beside the woman stood a cloth bag, stuffed with balls of yarn. Assorted colors peeked over the top and one long blue string snaked from the bag to the lady's fingers. In her other hand she wove a metal hook in and out of a square of yarn.

"I'm curious," I said as I walked over to her. "What exactly are you working on?"

She peeked at me over the rims of her trifocals. "This is crochet. I love to crochet. It gives me something to do while I wait for my children."

I sat next to her in a gold club chair – not quite so large a chair nor as intimidating as the wingback. "I've always admired people who do handicrafts. You're very good at crochet and really fast."

"Thank you. I'm making another afghan, for one of my grandchildren. I have five grandchildren, you know. They're coming to see me today."

"I'm so glad. You must be very excited. I love it when my son and his wife come to see me. By the way, my name is Reverend G."

"I'm Edith," she said, transferring the metal hook to her left hand and holding out her right hand to shake mine. I marveled that such a frail little hand moved so quickly with that crochet hook and the yarn.

"My children are coming today," she repeated. Edith

hooked the blue string of yarn again and wove it into the pattern. "Do you crochet?" she asked.

"Oh, no. I never had time to learn handicrafts, with all the busy-ness of the church, the needs of the people, weddings and funerals. But I think afghans are beautiful, and this is a lovely pattern you're working on."

"I could make one for you, if you'd like. Afghans feel so warm and comforting on cold winter evenings. I'm making this one for my grandson, Josh. He likes blue. He's coming to see me today." The hook and its attached string danced in her fingers. "What colors do you like?" she asked.

"Hmm. Well, my couch is sort of green and beige, kind of tweedy, you know. I have brown pillows on it that my daughter-in-love bought for me. Jessica. She's very good at picking out furniture and accessories. Maybe I'll ask her what color of afghan I should order from you, Edith. How much do you charge to make one?"

"Oh, no. I never charge for my projects. Crochet is something I love to do. It keeps my hands busy, and the doctor says I don't have a smidge of arthritis, because my hands are always active. Isn't that nice?"

I nodded. "It is indeed. None of us wants to have arthritis. Very painful."

Roxie walked toward us. "Oh, there you are, Reverend G. I need you for a minute, please."

I stood up and patted Edith's arm. "I hope to see you again, Edith. It was wonderful to meet such a talented lady."

She giggled and seemed embarrassed at the compliment. "Likewise. Nice to meet you." Edith wrapped the string of yarn and the piece of afghan together, then stuck the hook in the middle of another yarn ball. "I'd better get ready," she said. "My children will be here soon."

Roxie and I walked away from Edith. "That just burns me," Roxie said.

"What?"

"Edith. She sits there almost every day and waits for her family to come."

"But why does that upset you?"

Roxie stopped and faced me. Her cheeks turned redder as she spit out the words. "Because. That poor woman sits there for hours, works on her crochet and creates hundreds of afghans of all different colors. I go to Hobby Lobby and get the yarn for her, every two weeks. She keeps herself busy, just waiting and waiting for a family that never comes."

"You mean...she's expecting them and they're not coming today?"

"Not today. Not ever. Edith has lived here for three years and no one ever comes to see her. About a year ago, she started camping out in the lobby with her crochet bag and her yarn balls, just hoping against hope that someone would come — anyone. But they never do. Not for her birthday. Not for Christmas. Not even for stupid Mother's Day. They just never come."

Roxie's eyes filled with tears as her anger turned liquid. "I tell you, Reverend G. Some people get on my last nerve."

I patted her arm. "Poor Edith. Waiting there every day. How far away does her family live?"

Roxie looked at me as if I had lost my last noodle. "They live right here in Lawton Springs. Just a few miles away from Cove Creek, yet they don't care enough about that little woman to come see her for even five minutes. Sometimes I hate my job."

We stood outside the MC unit while Roxie pounded the numbers into the keypad. She must have missed a number or hit one of them twice, because the door refused to open. "Crap," she said. "I'm sorry, Reverend G. I shouldn't say that in front of you."

I rubbed her back. "Sweet Roxie, don't worry about it. You're having a rough day. God understands that."

"Yeah, well, my day is just about to get worse."

This time, the code worked and the door opened. We stopped outside Marie's room. I wondered if Marie felt agitated again and Roxie wanted me to pray for her. But as Roxie opened the door, I saw that Marie lay quietly in her bed, her eyes closed, her head still. Everything completely still. Curled up beside her was Gabriel, his left paw on Marie's hand.

Roxie spoke in clipped sentences. "The nurse called me a moment ago. She discovered Gabriel here, but didn't want to cause a scene. Marie is dead, and Gabriel has once again escaped from your room. Now, please take your cat back to your apartment while I make arrangements for Marie. We'll have to discuss what's going to happen to Gabriel later."

I picked up my cat and held him close, then I touched Marie's cold hand for a moment. We moved quickly toward the door, but I turned to look back. Roxie stood over Marie, stroked her hair and quietly cried.

"I'm sorry, Roxie," I said as I opened the door. Out in the hallway, I petted Gabriel's head, smoothed back his ears and listened to his responding purr.

"Oh, Gabriel. What are we going to do? You tried to comfort Marie as she moved from earth to heaven, but you shouldn't even be in her room. You're naughty and nice at the same time. How in the world are you getting out of our apartment and into Memory Care?"

Oh God, oh God, help us. Help us, please.

∾

Chris answered his phone on the second ring. He must have programmed my number into his Caller ID, because he said, "Tru? What's up?"

"Come help me, Chris. I'm in the middle of an emergency with Gabriel. I tried to call Jacob, but left a voice…thing, a voice whatever it's called."

"Voicemail?"

"Okay. Voicemail. A lady just died…I forget her name…a nice lady in the MC unit…I can't remember her name, but she died, and Gabriel was with her. He escaped again, and they're going to take him away. I just know it. Chris, can you come?"

"Let me finish one thing — for my class tomorrow, then I'll be there. Don't worry, Tru. Keep the faith. Everything will be all right."

"Thanks." I hung up the phone and cuddled with Gabriel. He responded with that same purr that always encouraged me. "I depend on you, dear Gabriel, to make me feel better when I'm lonely. When you cuddle with me at night, when you purr, it makes me warm all over. Just having you for company helps me. They can't take you away. I need you. Oh, why do you have to keep prowling around? Why can't you just stay put?"

God, please, please — don't let them take Gabriel away from me. I can't stand it. Maybe if I promise to keep him in his cat carrier and never let him out. But what kind of life is that? Gabriel locked up just like those poor souls in Memory Care? That's no way for a cat to live.

"Gabriel, I know what to do. Let's pray an animal blessing

over you. The Catholics do it all the time, and Father Francis over at Sacred Heart has a special ceremony every spring. People from all over town bring their animals for the blessing. Maybe if I call Father Francis…" I searched through the phone book while Gabriel groomed his south end. "Now what is the name of his church? Oh, God, help us. I'll have to wait until Chris or Jacob gets here and ask one of them."

I paced in my apartment for what seemed like hours although the clock marked it as ten minutes. Still, Chris didn't come, but neither did Roxie. Maybe she changed her mind and gave us a reprieve. Finally, the phone rang.

"Mom? What's wrong? Your voicemail sounded frantic."

"Oh, Jacob. It's terrible. A lady died and Gabriel was in the room when it happened and now they're going to take him away and he'll probably have to go to the pound and they'll put him to sleep. I can't stand it. I don't know what to do. I called Chris. He said he would come, but he isn't here yet."

Just then, a knock sounded on my door. "Oh, someone is here. Jacob, someone is knocking."

I hung up the phone and hurried to the door. Chris and Roxie stood there together. "Oh, dear," I said. "It's the campus police. I'm not guilty. Please don't take away my cat."

Chris came into the room and gently led me to my recliner. "Just relax, Tru. We'll get to the bottom of this."

Roxie exchanged a look with Chris, then she knelt beside the recliner and took my hand. "I'm sorry, Reverend G. With all my stress today — lots of things going on, then I saw Edith and felt so badly for her and then Marie died. I took it out on you and Gabriel."

"Marie," I said to Chris. "That's the lady who died. Marie."

Chris nodded, and Roxie continued. "Professor Jacobs

called me and said he was on his way. He asked me to meet him here in your apartment so we can talk about this. I'm so sorry I upset you."

I sighed and inhaled half the oxygen in the room. "It's all right, Honey. I understand. You do such good work here. I'm just so worried about Gabriel, and I can't for the life of me figure out how he escapes. I promise you that I close my door tightly every time I leave, unless my Sometimer's kicks in and I forget. But I don't think so. I know it's important to keep Gabriel a secret."

Chris put a finger to his lips and motioned for me to be quiet. Then he pointed toward the picture window on my south wall. I always kept the window open a couple of inches to let in fresh air, for my own health and because I knew Gabriel liked it. He often sat on the sill, just where he sat now.

The three of us watched as he picked at a corner of the outer window screen with his paw. Then he pushed out a tiny piece of the screen. He squeezed himself under the few inches of open window and out of that small opening in the screen. Within seconds, Gabriel jumped to the ground and moved across the grass toward the next wing.

"The little rascal," said Roxie.

"Now we know how he gets out of your apartment," Chris said. "But how does he manage to get back in?"

Like three police officers staking out a criminal, we stood at the window and watched Gabriel move stealthily across the grounds. A yellow butterfly distracted him, and he swiped at it, but missed and moved on. His striped tail stood at a perpendicular angle to his body, and he quickly covered the spaces between shrubs and outdoor plants. A patio table and chairs sat on colorful pavers. Gabriel jumped on the table, then the chair, then back to the mulched ground on the other side.

"Protecting his paws from those hot pavers," Chris said.

Gabriel slinked past other apartment windows and finally to the outside exit for the kitchen. Within minutes, one of the kitchen staff opened the door. He glanced around, then reached inside his pocket and pulled out a lighter and a cigarette.

"Smoker's break," said Roxie.

The worker closed his eyes and inhaled deeply. He never noticed the tortoiseshell cat that slipped into the kitchen before the door closed.

"Let's go," said Roxie. "Down the hallway to the kitchen. I hope he's not jumping on counters and eating food. The health inspector will have a fit."

We started toward my door just as it flew open. Jacob stood there, his face red, his cowlick standing straight up. "Mom. I came as soon as I could. Ran red lights and broke speed limits. What's wrong?"

I laughed. "Bless you, Jacob. Come along with us, and I'll explain. Gabriel is on another caper, and we're following him."

The four of us hurried into the hallway and down the adjoining wing, following Roxie's lead. We rushed through the dining room and toward the kitchen. I told Jacob how Gabriel slipped under my window and pushed out the screen, then waited until the kitchen exit door opened to slink inside.

"That's the emergency?" Jacob asked, puffing along beside me. "I thought you said someone died and they were taking Gabriel away from you."

"There he is," interrupted Chris, pointing toward the double doors of the kitchen. One of the staff carried dessert dishes of vanilla pudding in a tray. Close to her feet moved my crafty cat, who almost tripped the poor woman. Now at a faster pace, he moved away from the kitchen and toward another wing. His tail disappeared around the corner as we ran toward him.

We turned the corner and stopped. Jacob almost knocked me over. He grabbed my arm. All the doors in this wing were closed. No sign of Gabriel.

"Let's split up," Chris gasped, trying to catch his breath. "Check every room."

"No, wait," said Roxie. "I think I know which room he's in. I've been thinking about this for a while, and I have a theory. If I'm right, this will explain why Gabriel is so intent on escaping. Follow me."

We made a single file line behind her as Roxie headed toward the fourth apartment on the right. She knocked briefly, then opened the door and motioned for all of us to come in. An elderly man lay sleeping in the bed while a young woman stood at her feet. She dabbed at her eyes with a pink handkerchief.

Roxie moved toward her and put an arm around her shoulders. "How's Harold today? How's your daddy doing?"

The woman dabbed her eyes again and whispered. "The doctor just examined him. Not much time left for Daddy. Maybe not even a week."

Roxie held her close, then Harold's daughter spoke again. "When the doctor left, this cat walked in and jumped on the bed. It seems to comfort Daddy, so I don't have the heart to pick it up and move it. Do you know who it belongs to?"

Oh, yes, I wanted to say. I know whom he belongs to, for there lay Gabriel, curled up beside Harold, his left paw on Harold's arm.

chapter 10

The four of us sat in my apartment and munched on the cheesecake Roxie "borrowed" from the kitchen. "No one will miss four pieces," she said as she served us on yellow paper plates. She topped mine with blueberries.

"Perfect," I said, and took a big, juicy bite.

Roxie settled into my recliner and stabbed her cheesecake with a fork. "Now that Gabriel is finished running around, let's talk. Again, I'm sorry, Reverend G, for my anger earlier today and for being so dogmatic about your cat. When we found Gabriel in Harold's room, it sort of confirmed something I've been thinking about."

She stood up and handed a folder to Jacob. "You can see I've collected some information about this subject."

Jacob opened the folder, pulled out a magazine article and read, "Local cat warns residents of impending death. Director of assisted living puts cat on staff list."

"What?" Chris said. "A cat on the staff? Do they pay him?"

I snickered and finished my cheesecake, licking the fork. Gabriel napped beside me, exhausted from his run through the hallways. A giant piece of duct tape crisscrossed the screen where he escaped earlier. Chris and Jacob taped the screen as soon as we all came back to my apartment.

"It's true," said Roxie, "an assisted living place in some town in Rhode Island. This cat has a gift for sensing impending death in the residents. The human body releases certain toxins and/or chemicals as death approaches. The cat smells the chemicals and warns the staff by showing up in that particular resident's room."

Jacob scanned the article. "It says here that the director really appreciates this cat, because it gives her time to call in the family. They say their good-byes, make some arrangements, et cetera while there's still time. Everyone is more prepared when the death comes."

Chris finished his cheesecake and put his empty plate on the coffee table. "But what about the person who's about to die? Wouldn't it be rather frightening to be visited by the Death Cat?"

Again, Jacob read portions of the article. "That question is addressed here. According to the director, most of the residents already exist in a coma or a semi-conscious state. They aren't even aware that the cat, whose name is Toby, has given the signal of impending death. In one case where the woman was conscious, Toby's warning gave her time to say her good-byes and even make restitution with an estranged family member."

"Right," said Roxie. "I can see that as a possibility and a comfort to the entire family. According to what I've read, the staff never makes a big deal out of it when Toby arrives. They quietly go about their work, make the resident comfortable and warn the family that there's a strong possibility their family member is about to pass away."

I sat forward. "So, Roxie, you think Gabriel might have this gift, that he can sense impending death?"

"Look at the evidence. He curled up next to Annie, just a week before she died. Then he found his way into the MC unit to Marie. She died a few days afterward. Today, he targeted Harold, who we know is terminal. So far, Gabriel is batting a thousand."

"Amazing," said Chris.

"What a smart cat!" I added, stroking Gabriel's back. He opened one eye, yawned and settled back down for another nap. "Tired kitty. You scoped out Harold's room, jumped on the bed and quietly let him know he has little time left. You've had a busy day."

Jacob, always the practical one, handed Roxie's info back to her. "So what's the next step? How do we integrate Gabriel into the life of Cove Creek as the Cat of Death? Are there any legal issues we need to be aware of?"

"Not that I know of," Roxie stacked all the dirty plates and carried them to my kitchen trash can. "I'll talk to the head director, of course, and we'll call a staff meeting. For now, we don't need to do anything, especially since we have Gabriel's escape hole taped up. I'll call maintenance tomorrow and tell them to replace the screen. Actually, I think this whole idea about Gabriel's gift is a comfort."

"You mean for the family?" asked Chris as he stood up.

"Not just for them, but for all of us." Roxie cleared her throat. "You may not realize how difficult it is for us, the staff, when we lose a resident. We love our people here at Cove Creek. We learn about their stories, their families, their likes and dislikes. We truly care about them, and when death takes them away — we grieve. You never see it, because we're professionals and we hide it. But sometimes, I want to scream from the pain of working around constant death. Sometimes, I hate this job. If Gabriel makes it easier, then I'm all for it."

With that statement, Roxie left.

Chris stood quietly beside the sofa while Jacob studied the floor. I petted Gabriel and wished life was easier for all the people at Cove Creek.

You told us, Lord, that death would have no sting when we put our hope in you. But it sure stings a lot for those of us left behind. It stings for Roxie and the staff, for the grieving families and for those of us who face a terminal illness. Death isn't easy, Lord. Help us to understand, and thank you for letting me keep Gabriel.

∽

Chaplain Pete finished Harold's funeral with words from the Gospel of John, "I am the resurrection and the life. He who believes in me shall live, even if he dies.'" Pete closed his Bible and tucked it under his arm. "Harold believed these words, and he believed in Jesus, so he's more alive now than ever before. Let's remember this truth and keep our focus on the heavenly life to come."

As we filed out of the pews, I noticed Bert wiping tears from his face. Probably thinking about Annie and missing her all over again. The heaviness of the day and the loss of another Cove Creek resident seemed to hang over the chapel. Roxie stood at the back of the room, helped people move their walkers in the right direction, acted like a professional and hid her grief. I wished I knew how to help her feel better, but for now — I needed to talk to Pete.

"Can you join me in the dining room, Pete? I'd like to chat with you a minute."

"Sure," he said, as he closed his Bible and gathered his papers. "What did you think about the service? Was it okay?

I barely knew Harold, but I tried to get some interesting information from his family."

"Great job, Pete. You made Harold's service personal and sweet. I'm sure the family felt comforted, and as always, your music sounded terrific."

We settled ourselves around one of the round tables. I noticed Meredith at another table, with papers spread out between her and Charlotte. They seemed to be in an animated conversation. Charlotte seemed almost…ecstatic? She pointed to a page and explained something to Meredith. Was that the beginning of a smile on Charlotte's face?

"So, what's up?" asked Pete.

I scooched my chair a little closer. "This is kind of a secret, but I wanted to let you in on it, as another minister. Roxie is still checking up on the legalities, but everything should be good to go, really soon."

Pete looked puzzled. "Legalities? What's going on?"

"Well, as you know, I own a cat and it seems that my cat, Gabriel, is gifted. He smells the chemicals bodies give off before people die."

"He smells what?"

"Oh, don't look at me like that, Pete. I'm not crazy. I just have dementia or Alzheimer's or whatever — it doesn't matter. I'm telling you the truth. Roxie can show you the research about it, if you want. Gabriel smells the residents' chemicals and predicts who is going to die."

Pete looked around the room. "Where is Roxie? Maybe we should include her in this conversation."

"She's busy, and I'm not crazy. Gabriel knows how to target the next person headed for eternity. Roxie says that when Gabriel shows up, the staff notifies the family that their loved one is destined for another world. Isn't that a comfort? Well, here's where we come in. You and I watch for Gabriel's sign, then we offer support and encouragement for the family and the staff. You know, just be present in the room and help any way we can — the ministry of presence. What do you think?"

He picked up his Bible and stood. Then he leaned toward me. "You and I? We offer support for the family? You sound as if we're teammates or co-ministers on staff here. I don't like this, Reverend G. It smacks of sensationalism. I think you're still trying to be a minister when it's clear your working days ended some time ago. I think you should completely forget about this idea." He pushed his chair toward the table and walked briskly out of the room.

"Well, okay. If that's what you think," I said to the back of his suit. "Don't go away mad. Just go away." I sat at the table for a while and thought about Pete's words.

Trying to be a minister...working days over...sensationalism. That's what Pete said? Sensationalism. All I'm trying to do is help, Lord. That's all. Maybe I am trying to make myself feel better and discover a new purpose here. Am I inventing this? Should I just leave people alone? Can I still be your servant, Lord? Maybe Pete is wrong, and I'm right. I don't know.

"I have loved you with an everlasting love."

Thanks, Lord. I love you, too, but I still long to comfort these people and their families. I miss the ministry, Lord. I want to help others. Show me, Lord. Teach me. Help me to be a helper or show me how to let it go.

Meredith's colorful scarf caught my eye and added variety to my bleak thoughts. I watched her relate to Charlotte who seemed to enjoy their time together. Charlotte pointed to something on one page while Meredith nodded. Then Meredith glanced at me and gave me a thumbs-up sign. I returned it with a smile and a prayer of thanksgiving.

∽

Jacob and Jessie faced me across the booth at Pizza Hut. We ordered a large pepperoni with extra cheese and watched the waitress balance our salad plates on her way to our table. I finished my salad while Jessie picked at her lettuce. She looked a little distracted, and I wondered what was on her mind. Maybe she disliked the broccoli on top of her lettuce mountain or maybe she wanted to save room for the pizza. Maybe a bad day at school. No, wait. This was summer. Jessie never worked during the summer.

Oh, God, I'm having trouble staying on track today. Help me not to lose my mind in front of my beloved children. The waitress will throw me out of this place and never let me come back. I can't stand it.

"I can't stand it," Jacob echoed my thoughts. "Jess, I can't wait for the pizza."

She squeezed his arm. "Oh, go ahead. I'm finished with my salad anyway."

Jacob put his arm around Jessie and kissed her cheek. Then he turned toward me with a funny grin on his face. "Remember several weeks ago, Mom? We mentioned that we were going to a counselor and we had a special timeline?"

"No. Sorry, I don't remember that. You're seeing a counselor? Why?"

Oh, God, my children are having some sort of problem. Is it my fault? What did I miss?

They looked at each other, then Jessie reached for my hand. "It doesn't matter now, because we've worked through the problem and we're doing great. We don't want to worry you with the details."

"But if you've been seeing a counselor, then I should be worried, right? That means something is terribly wrong, and I hope to God it isn't because of me and this stupid forgetfulness. Because if it is my fault, then please forgive me. I apologize already."

"Mom, please." Jacob sat forward. "Let's get back on track. Forget that I said anything about the counseling. That conversation is over. We want to tell you something else, and I didn't start off very well." He looked at Jessie and kissed her again. "We're pregnant, Mom. We're going to have a baby. Your first grandchild. Sooner than we planned, but we're so excited. Doc Sanders confirmed it today."

I looked back and forth between my beloved son and my daughter-in-love. So Jessie couldn't finish her salad because of her pregnancy and the raging hormones. I remembered my own morning sickness — which actually lasted all day. I ate nothing but dry Cheerios for three months. Anything connected with meat or grease sent me immediately to the bathroom. I worried that Jacob might be brain damaged from lack of protein or born with an intense craving for little bites of dry cereal.

"Pregnant," I finally managed to say. "A baby. Oh, my goodness, my goodness. Bless you. Thank you, God. When? When is our baby due?"

Jessie giggled and snuggled closer to Jacob. "Sometime around the middle of April. I hoped to teach the entire school year, but this will work out fine. A sub can handle my class for the month of May, and then I'll recuperate during the summer."

"Good plan," I said. "Wonderful plan. You can bring the baby to Cove Creek and all of us old folks will ooh and ah."

"You're not old," said Jacob, "and of course, we'll bring the baby to see you."

"Oh. I'll ask Edith if she'll crochet a baby blanket for you. She loves to crochet. Should it be pink or blue?"

"A crocheted blanket sounds nice," said Jessie, while a soft glow lightened her eyes. "How about a pale yellow? We don't know yet if it's a boy or a girl, but I want to do a yellow theme in the nursery."

"Yellow it is. Always a cheerful color." I sipped my iced tea just as the waitress plopped the pizza on our table. "Pepperoni? I don't remember ordering pepperoni. I think I wanted cream cheese with ham and pineapple."

Jacob's happy face suddenly darkened. "We talked about it, Mom. You said pepperoni was fine."

"I did? Well, okay. I'll just pick those little circles off and eat it without the meat. How about you, Jessie? Do you want extra meat? You can have mine." I stabbed one of the pepperoni's with my fork and handed it to her.

"No, thanks," she said. "In fact…Jacob…let me out of the booth. I need to go to the restroom. Hurry."

Jacob scooted out and watched Jessie run toward the back of the restaurant.

I took a big bite and said, "What's wrong with her?"

∽

On my daily walk, Roxie suddenly joined me. "I'll walk with you, Reverend G. I need the exercise anyway, plus I want to tell you something."

"Great. Glad to have the company. Did I tell you that my beloved children are pregnant? Due in April."

"Yes, you told me yesterday. That's wonderful news."

"I'm going to ask that lady who likes to crochet if she'll make a baby blanket. What was her name?"

"Edith. Her name is Edith and she lives in the same wing as you. She's sitting in the lobby again today. You might want to visit with her when you finish your walk."

We marched along in silence for a while, then Roxie said, "I talked to the director and all the legal eagles about Gabriel. We decided to quietly let him use his gift, but we won't make any big deal out of it. If Gabriel chooses someone to…uhm… visit, then we'll call in the medical staff to confirm whether the person is close to death. If so, we'll contact the family, but we don't want any press about this. People in the community might get the wrong idea."

I nodded. "Sounds like a good plan. So Gabriel stays with me, and we won't get into any trouble if he slips out the door?"

"Of course he stays with you," Roxie slipped her arm around my waist. "We've checked all the screens throughout the facility and yours is now brand new. If Gabriel slips out, we'll assume he's on duty, and we'll follow him."

Thank you, God, for working this out. I do love this cat, but I hated the idea of Gabriel causing a problem. Bless Roxie for all her practical help and for understanding how much I need my cat.

"One other thing, Reverend G. The chaplain talked to me the other day about your idea to follow Gabriel and minister to the residents."

"Yes. Don't you think that's a good idea – for Chaplain Pete or me to go to the room and comfort the person?"

Roxie shook her head. "When a person nears death, we want to help them, of course. We try to make them as comfortable as possible and if the family requests a chaplain or a minister, then we comply with that request. But Reverend G, you can't just go into the rooms and offer your services. We can't allow that. You're a wonderful person, but here at Cove Creek, you're just a resident. Please remember that. Okay?"

"Okay." I felt like an errant child, disciplined by our precious activities director. The staff at Cove Creek refused my offer of ministry to residents and their families. Reverend G — not allowed to comfort people who faced death, to pray with them and act as a minister of the Gospel. But isn't that what Christians do…help each other…especially during the difficult times of life and death?

Roxie clearly stated the truth. I was only a resident, not a minister. I knew that fact in my addled brain, but my heart still wanted to help — as long as possible. It wasn't easy to turn off the ministry button and tune out of life. On the other hand, Roxie needed to do her job and consider all the legal ramifications. Wonderful, patient Roxie.

Help me to swallow my pride, Lord, and what is left of my call to minister. But this is not going to be easy. Help me, Lord. Love me, please. Bring comfort to this old minister's heart. I'm feeling rejected again, and I hate to cry, right here in front of our activities director.

Roxie steered me toward the front lobby. "Here we are, and here is Edith."

"Hello," I said. "What are we doing in the lobby with this woman?"

Roxie prompted. "Weren't you going to ask her about the baby afghan?"

"Oh, yes. Thank you for reminding me, and thank you for walking with me, dear." I blinked away my tears, moved closer to Edith and sat in one of the club chairs beside her. A purple strand flowed out of her tapestry bag and wove itself between her fingers, forming a beautiful square of color in her hand.

"Edith, my children are expecting a baby. Next spring, I think. Could you make a yellow baby blanket for them? I think they wanted yellow. Yes, I'm sure. That soft, baby yellow. Or maybe Jessie said something about green. I don't know. Surprise me. I'll pay you for the yarn."

The purple strand stopped for a moment as Edith looked toward me. "Of course, I would love to make a baby blanket. But you don't have to pay me. I have lots of yarn." She reached into her bag and pulled out a ball of pastel yellow with tiny flecks of turquoise. "How about this one? Is this the right color?"

"Perfect." I touched the ball. Soft as a baby's cheek. My grandbaby's cheek. Suddenly, the joy of the moment overcame me, and I started to cry. Imagine that! A baby on the way for Jacob and Jessie, a little one to hold and tell about the Jesus story and cuddle close. A new baby to join our family.

Edith started empathy crying. For several moments we sat there, sniffing and weeping together as Edith continued to weave her purple strands. Finally, her voice cracked as she said, "My children are coming today. They should be here soon."

∽

Jacob sat next to me in Doc Sanders exam room. "It seems to be getting worse, Doc." Jacob said. "The memory lapses are shorter. Even within the same conversation. Don't you think so, Mom?"

"I don't know. I feel okay. Sometimes I get confused, but sometimes I feel right on top of things. Do you think I'm crazy?"

Jacob shook his head. "No, not crazy. I just wonder if Doc can prescribe something to help. I'm worried about you, Mom, and with the baby coming — I want you to enjoy being a grandmother." He looked toward Doc Sanders who quietly wrote in a manila folder.

Oh, God, help me. I want to be a good grandmother. Please help me not to turn into a loony-tune. Please give wisdom to Doc Sanders.

"Hope in God. Stay in hope."

But where is the hope, Lord, when Jacob says I'm worse? I've noticed the worry on Jessie's face. And what does Chris think? Where is Chris? I haven't seen him for a while. Is he avoiding me? Is he afraid of being with a demented old woman?

"I love you. Trust me."

Thanks, Lord. I love you, too, but I'm afraid. By the way, where is Chris? Is he all right? Why haven't I seen him for a while?

Doc put his folder on the table and nodded at Jacob. "I'm glad you're worried about your mother. It shows you care a great deal about her. Unfortunately, there isn't really a standard formula for dealing with dementia or with early-onset Alzheimer's. Everyone progresses through the disease at a different rate. Time and space usually regress first. How are you doing with time, Reverend? Do you know what day this is?"

"Sure. It's August third." I glanced at Doc's wall calendar. "Tuesday."

"Yes, and what day of the week is tomorrow? Do you remember the days when you're alone in your apartment, when you don't have my calendar to look at?"

Rats. He caught me. "Of course, I remember. Thursday is

RJ THESMAN

Bingo Day. Friday, we have chapel. On Mondays, I meet with the chaplain and we discuss what he's going to talk about the next Friday. Every day, I take a walk. Jacob showed me how to mark off the days on my calendar."

"Mark off the days?"

Jacob shifted in his chair. "I noticed that Mom forgets the days, sometimes." He patted my hand. "Not always. So I bought her a calendar and showed her how to mark off each day with a big X before she goes to bed. Then she knows when she gets up, what the new day is. It seems to help."

"Well, if she can remember to do that task, then I'm not too concerned. That's a good system, by the way. I'll suggest it to some of my other patients."

Lord, they're talking around me, as if I no longer exist. They think I'm sitting here in the third person and I don't understand. Do they really care about me? I don't like this, God. Please help me.

Doc continued. "A new drug on the market seems to help with alertness. I'm going to give you a prescription, but leave it with the nurses at Cove Creek. It's their job to get it filled and administer it every day."

Oh, Lord, I'm going to be one of those little old ladies that gets a Dixie cup at lunch with medicines hidden inside. Pretty soon, I'll act as cuckoo as Grandpa. Then they'll move me to the MC unit, like Marie, where I'll disappear into myself. I can't stand this.

"Do you understand, Reverend G?" Doc spoke to me again.

"Sure. Take my medicine like a good girl and try not to act crazy."

"Yes, take your medicine but also, relax and enjoy each day. Meet new people. Try new activities. Stay as active as possible. Keep walking every day. You're actually doing very well." Doc ripped a sheet from his script pad and handed it to Jacob. "I want to see her again in two months. We'll see if these meds help or if we need to try something else."

I just want to leave. Get me out of here, Lord. Out of this office and out of this mess. Take me home to heaven, please. No, wait — I want to see my grandbaby first. I need nine more months. It is nine, isn't it?

"Let's go, Mom." Jacob steered me toward the door. "How about an ice cream cone?"

I am not a child that you can pacify with ice cream. Do not treat me like a child.

I turned back toward Doc Sanders. "How is your wife, Doc? I remember you told me she also lives at Cove Creek. How can I pray for her and for you?"

He seemed surprised that I remembered this particular fact. "She's about the same, but thank you for asking. Yes, please pray for her. Pray for both of us."

"Absolutely. Prayer is something I still do, thankfully." I tried to stand up to my full height and show some dignity. "Now, my darling son, how about some Chunky Monkey? Not a cone. I need a quart, all to myself."

chapter 11

A week or two later, I admitted that I felt better. The medicine gave me a little buzz at first and kept me awake at night, so I crawled out of bed and opened my Bible to some of my favorite Psalms. Gabriel cuddled next to me on the sofa and listened to me read.

"He who dwells in the shelter of the Most High will abide in the shadow of the Almighty."

Keep me in your shelter, Lord. Please let me stay so close to you that I live in your shadow. I want your arms around me. I want to dwell with you.

"You will not be afraid of the terror by night, or of the arrow that flies by day; of the pestilence that stalks in darkness, or of the destruction that lays waste at noon."

But I am afraid, Lord. It's night time, and I can't sleep. I'm sitting here alone, reading your words to my cat, who seems to have no trouble at all sleeping. I am afraid.

Gabriel stretched out his front legs and settled down for a new version of his cat nap.

I live in the middle of destruction, Lord, the destruction of my mind. I did not ask for this. I'd rather struggle through some sort of physical illness, something a surgeon cuts out of me or medicates away, rather than this destructive monster of the mind. I want to be young again, Lord, full of energy and vitality. I want to think about new ideas, new ministries and all sorts of new sermon topics. All I do now is live one day after the other, mark the days off on my calendar and pray for your help. Be my refuge and my fortress. Help me, Lord.

The sweet baritone of the Lord answered, "I will be with you in trouble. I will rescue you and honor you. With a long life, I will satisfy you and let you behold my salvation. I am the Lord your God who rescues you. Stay in hope."

But I hate the idea of a long life if it continues like this, one demented day after another. Thank you for the medicine that helps me feel better, Lord, but now I realize the extent of this disease. With this new medicine, I recognize more of my mistakes. Do you realize, Lord, that today I ate a handful of Gabriel's cat food? I stuck it in my mouth without thinking. Without thinking, Lord. That's the problem. I no longer think. What do you say about that?

No answer. Silence in my soul.

Never leave me alone, Lord. I need you so much. Please, I can't stand it.

"I will never leave you. I will never forsake you. I am with you always, even to the end of the world."

Never forsake me. Never leave me, but how do I make it through this night?

"In everything give thanks. Trust me."

I bowed my head and petted Gabriel. *Thank you for this cat beside me, Lord, and for his warm body. Thank you that Gabriel lives with me and loves me with an unconditional love. Thank you for your unconditional love, too. I can do nothing to earn your love. It's just there, always and always.*

Thank you for my wonderful son and his beautiful Jessie

and for the grandbaby. A baby, Lord. Thank you for this child and for something wonderful to look forward to. Thank you for Roxie and the staff here at Cove Creek who love us and take such good care of us. Thank you for the medicines they give us, and thank you for the good food, especially when we have cheesecake with blueberries.

Thank you for Chaplain Pete and Edith and the baby afghan she works on. Thank you again for the baby. I can hardly wait to see if she looks like my beloved Jacob. I hope she doesn't sprout a cowlick. No fun for a girl. Thank you, God. You already know about her hair, the color of her eyes and how tall she will be when full-grown. Or he, Lord. Maybe a boy to play football or pole vault at the track meets. Maybe another whiz kid like Jacob who understands calculus and algebra. You already know if he will make incredible science projects or compose music or do both. Will he have his mother's eyes and her tender personality? A baby, Lord. Thank you, thank you.

And thank you for my best friend, Chris. By the way, I haven't seen him forever. Where is he?

∞

I walked past the courtyard and noticed a man, bent over with a hoe in his hand. Was that Bert? Hard to tell from his backside, but I knew Bert planned to work in the courtyard.

"Could you open the door for me, Roxie? Is that Bert out there?"

"Yes. Go see what he's doing. It's amazing." She coded in the numbers and gave the door a shove. "You have company, Bert. About twenty more minutes before snack time."

Someone had tilled the east end of the courtyard and

removed the old shrubs. Three tomato plants stood in one corner, surrounded by marigolds. A row of purple petunias outlined the north side, adding color to the bland mulch. Along the walkway stood a large wooden structure, divided into smaller squares.

"Bert," I called, trying not to look at his bent over back end. "How have you been, my friend?"

He straightened up, leaned on the hoe and smiled. "If I was any better, I'd have ta' take somethin' for it." He pulled a red bandanna handkerchief out of his side pocket and wiped his face. "What do ya' think about my garden? Lookee there," he said, pointing to the orange-colored plants. "I got some mary-golds for Annie."

"They're wonderful, Bert, and I love the purple petunias. They look great around the border of the plot. But what is this wooden thing in the middle?"

"That's called Square Foot Gardenin'. Roxie looked it up on that there Google thing. It's a raised box, so anyone who wants to can plant somethin' in their square, without even bendin' over. Then I water it every day and pick out the weeds. Hey, you wanta' plant somethin'? I got some starters right over here." Bert pointed to a pile of mulch at the west end of the courtyard. Beside it stood a crate of tiny plants, yellows and oranges and purples.

He walked with me toward the plants. "It's gettin' on in the plantin' season this year, but we can still do mums or asters or them late daisies. Pick out what ya' want. Whew! It's hot enough out here for the trees to start chasin' the dogs."

I looked at the plants and chose a flower that seemed to lift its friendly face toward me. Tiny yellow tips bordered a dark salmon petal with a chestnut brown center. "I choose you," I said as I lifted it out of the crate.

Bert nodded his head. "That there is called the Indian Blanket flower. It's one of them flowers, you know, that comes back every year."

"A perennial?"

"Perennial, by cracky. That's what it is. That's the word."

Thank you, Lord. I actually remembered a word that Bert forgot. Maybe that new medicine really does help. Perennial. Indian Blanket is a perennial. Don't forget.

"I had no idea you were such an expert on flowers, Bert. I knew you farmed, but I didn't realize you were a botanist."

Another big word from somewhere in my brain. Botanist. Thank you, Lord. Perennial. Botanist. My words for the day.

Bert chuckled and handed me what looked like a tiny pitchfork. "I ain't no such thing as a botanist, but I've been studyin' catalogs Roxie gives me. Plus, Annie used to tell me all about her flowers." Bert used a tiny shovel to scoop some potting soil into one of the square foot boxes, then he helped me empty my Indian Blanket into the box and surround its roots with mulch.

"Let's pray for the planting, Bert."

"What?"

"In my church, we used to help the farmers prepare for the sowing months with a prayer service. You know, pray for good weather, for protection around the machinery, that sort of thing. Then later, we celebrated harvest season with a big potluck dinner. Everyone brought a pumpkin or a squash or a wreath made of wheat, and we thanked God for the harvest."

"Well now, that's a right good idea."

"So, let's you and I pray for this planting."

Bert took off his straw hat and his gloves. He bowed his

head over the raised garden as I began the old farmer's prayer from Saint Joseph, "Almighty God, who rules the seasons, we beseech thee so that our fields being safe from pests and favored by the weather may yield abundant crops. Thus freed from earthly worries may we after your example apply all our thoughts to eternal life…"

Was that the entire prayer? Add on a few words, just in case. "And P.S. God – Thank you for my good friend, Bert, and thank you for this wonderful garden. Thank you for Roxie and how she helped Bert with this project. Help us to remember, every time we see these flowers and vegetables, that you are the creator who made all these good things. Amen."

"Amen," echoed Bert, "and please, sir, say hello to my Annie."

∽

"So you see, Samson had all this massive hair, and that's where his strength came from. But he let his weakness over-power his strength."

Chaplain Pete stepped from behind the pulpit to illustrate his point. "Samson's weakness revolved around his lust for beautiful women. Instead of obeying God, he spent time with ungodly women and ended up in a terrible mess."

I was so proud of Pete. He took my advice to "Simplify the message" and redesigned his sermons into stories. Each week, Pete kept the messages simple, yet interesting. More and more of the residents joined us for chapel, then told others about their favorite chaplain.

Pete continued. "I brought my daughter with me today, to illustrate what happened to Samson. Now, Abby here will be Samson, and I will pretend to be Delilah." A young girl with a long blonde braid stood up in the front row and moved toward the stage.

"Look at that little sweetheart," Edith said as she poked me with her finger. Several other residents smiled and pointed. We loved to see children, especially our own children or grandchildren. We welcomed all the children who visited Cove Creek and treated them like long-lost treasures. Children's choirs sometimes came to sing on Sunday afternoons. The chapel always filled with residents who wanted to see and hear the little ones. I suppose the kiddos reminded us of our own childhoods — long disappeared into decades past. Pete was smart to bring his daughter with him today. I wondered how she would portray Samson.

Bert turned around in the pew in front of me. "I remember when my daughter was nigh onto that age. She had long hair, too, 'cept hers was dark black – like mine. Can ya' b'lieve I used to have black hair?"

"Shh," said Edith. "The chaplain's talking."

Pete motioned Abby into a chair in front of him, then he pulled out a long pair of scissors. "Now, don't be afraid," he said. "This is just an illustration, and Abby agreed to it. This is exactly what Samson let Delilah do to him."

To the horrified amazement of everyone, Chaplain Pete whacked that beautiful braid right off that child's head. Her new hairdo of short blonde strands fell into her face.

Charlotte jumped up and yelled, "Abuse. That's what it is. Child abuse. Someone send for the police."

Edith cried while another resident in the front row screamed, "Oh, baby."

"No, no," said Pete. "Abby grew her hair on purpose, to

give it to Locks of Love. They donate hair to cancer patients. It's all right. Everyone just relax."

But Charlotte had already thunked herself out the door to summon the authorities. "Police," we heard her scream. "Call the police."

Edith reached into her bag of yarn and pulled out the crochet needle. She held it in front of my nose. "Should I go up there with my hook and jab the chaplain?"

"I don't think so, Edith. Just relax. See? The child is okay."

Roxie hurried into the chapel with Charlotte beside her who pointed her cane toward Pete and cried, "Look there. See what he's done to that little child?"

Bert stood on the stage and comforted Abby whose face turned red during all the commotion. He patted her shoulder and tried to keep the chaplain away from his own daughter.

Roxie talked to several of the residents and motioned to everyone to be quiet, but it didn't work. Residents shouted or pointed toward Abby and Chaplain Pete. Staff from the kitchen and other offices stormed into the chapel to help. Different colors of scrubs contrasted with the dark wood of the pews.

Charlotte pointed her cane at the blonde braid that Abby now held in her lap. "He cut that child's hair right off. See? It's abuse, I tell you. Physical abuse."

I sat in the pew and laughed until my sides ached. Charlotte sneered at me.

The residents finally settled down and moved toward the doorway. They shook their heads and pointed at Chaplain Pete. Roxie escorted Bert off the stage while the rest of the staff helped residents with walkers and wheelchairs.

Ten minutes later, Chaplain Pete, Roxie, Abby and I sat alone in the chapel. For relaxation, Roxie taught us a couple of deep breathing exercises. "In through the nose," she said, "and slowly out through the mouth."

I patted Abby's shoulder. "What a wonderful thing to do, Sweetheart. Give your hair to Locks of Love."

The poor child nodded, but said nothing. Sweet little girl. Probably traumatized by a bunch of old folks who attacked her papa.

The chaplain shook his head. "I'm sorry, Roxie. I had no idea everyone would go ballistic over a planned haircut."

Roxie grinned at Pete. "It's all right, Pete. Everything is back to normal. Just don't bring scissors again, unless you check with me first."

"Well, one thing's for sure," I said. "None of us will ever forget the story of Samson and Delilah."

∽

"You have visitors," Roxie said as she pushed open my door. Beside her stood a beautiful woman with chocolate brown skin. A young boy peeked at me from behind Roxie's scrubs while a little girl with tiny dreadlocks grinned and showed the gap where her two front teeth used to be. The child wore a red calico dress with sequined flip-flops on her feet.

The mother walked gracefully around Roxie and came forward to shake my hand. "I'm Marinda, and these are my two children — Michael and Sharise. We rent your house and wanted to meet you."

"Oh, I'm so glad you did. Please, have a seat. Would you like something to drink?"

Roxie quietly closed the door as Marinda and her children arranged themselves on my sofa. The children were as beautiful as their mother with soft brown skin that glowed with youth and vitality, shiny black hair and almond-colored eyes.

The boy, Michael, spoke first. "Do you have Coke? I'd like a Coke."

His mother poked him with her elbow. "Please," he responded. "Please, may I have a Coke?"

"Absolutely. You, too, Sharise? And what about you, Marinda? What will you have?"

"Water, please, and Sharise can drink from mine."

I plunked ice cubes in the glasses, included one for myself, and poured the Coke. It fizzed all the way to the sofa.

Michael said, "Thank you" as I set his glass on the coffee table in front of him. All four of us sipped our drinks while I silently thanked God that my old house now provided a home for such a sweet family.

Thank you, God, for my Jacob, who did a fine job and chose this gracious woman and her children to live in my house. Bless them all, Lord.

Marinda started the conversation. "We've planned to come over and visit for a while, but we needed to get settled into the house and the neighborhood. Your son helped us paint the rooms and fix up a few things. I hope you don't mind the changes we've made."

"No, of course not. I'm never going back to that house, and I'm thrilled that you have such a sturdy roof over your heads. I lived as a single mom, too, after my husband died. I know how hard it is."

Hurray for Jacob. He helped this young family without taking any credit for it. He never told me how he painted rooms and repaired things at the old house — unless, of course, I forgot that I knew about it. I imagined Jacob on a ladder as he rolled a new color onto those old walls. I loved him all over again.

"You know, Marinda, we love our children no matter what they do. We love them when they make mistakes and when they do things right. No matter what — we love them because they're ours, and they own our hearts. But when we hear from someone else about something wonderful they've done — well, it just makes us mothers so proud. Don't you think?"

Marinda's eyes moistened, and I wondered how long she had parented all by herself. "I never expected to be a single mother," she said. "The divorce took me completely by surprise. I work two and sometimes three jobs at a time, just to keep food on the table. My children mean everything to me."

I reached over to stroke her arm. "I know. My Jacob and I share an incredible bond because of all the years we spent together, just the two of us. I'm sure you're doing a great job with your children."

Michael seemed bored by the intimate conversation. He looked around my apartment, probably for some sort of game. I wished I owned something to entertain him. Maybe the TV, except I hated to visit with someone over the noise of the television. No toys in my apartment. Too bad. I would need some when my grandbaby came. Remember: take the shuttle to Wal-Mart and buy some toys for the baby. Don't forget. Toys for the baby.

Sharise sat quietly beside her mother, occasionally sharing the glass of water. Suddenly, she bolted forward with a big smile on her face. "Kitty," she said, as she pointed toward my bedroom door.

Gabriel strolled into the room, stretched his front legs and yawned. Then he headed straight for Sharise and bounded onto her lap. Michael stood up and moved beside Sharise where they both petted Gabriel, stroked his fur and played with his tail.

"Oh, my," said Marinda. "Is it okay if the children pet your cat?"

"Of course. His name is Gabriel, and he loves the attention."

"Just be gentle," Marinda told her children. She scooted closer toward my chair. "I wanted you to know how much we appreciate everything. The rent is so reasonable, and the utilities manageable. As well as working full time, I'm also earning a degree — online. I plan to be an elementary teacher."

"Congratulations. I know how difficult it is to work, be a mother and also study. It takes a great deal of …"

What was that word? Work? No, that's not it. Lord, help me. Marinda waited.

What in the world was that word? "I'm sorry. I just lost my train of thought…motivation. That's the word. It takes a great deal of motivation to work and go to school and still be a good mom. You should be proud of yourself, dear."

"I guess I am, but I also know God helps us every day." Her eyes grew misty again, and I handed her the box of Kleenex. "You see, we never attended church when I was married. We were too busy. My husband worked on weekends while I took care of the babies. I wanted to be a stay-at-home mom. All my life, that's what I wanted. To be like my mother and stay at home with my babies."

She cleared her throat and dabbed at her eyes. "But after the divorce, when everything seemed so hard, I found my way to your church. In fact, we visited on that last day you were there — for your retirement party. Everybody celebrated with you, but some of the people still found time to greet us. They were so friendly, so nice."

Did I see Marinda and her children that Sunday? I only remembered the cheesecake and all the people who came to say good-bye. Cheesecake with lots of different toppings, but not this beautiful woman and her children.

Lord, I so hate this dementia.

Marinda smiled. "One woman, in particular, came over to me and seemed to genuinely welcome us. Her name was Mrs. Simmons. Mrs. Edna Simmons. I'll never forget her."

"Mrs. Simmons? About five foot eight, gray hair, little spirals all over her head?" The same Mrs. Simmons who vomited criticisms of me and sent those inflammatory emails?

"Yes, that's her. She invited us over to her house for supper that week, and she's the one who called your son when I told her we needed a place to live."

Well, God, here's another miracle. Mrs. Simmons acted nice to someone when I thought her entire purpose revolved around criticism. Strange that I remember everything about Mrs. Simmons but not an important word like "motivation."

Marinda continued. "Mrs. Simmons invited me to the women's retreat and that's where I met your daughter-in-law, Jessie. She helped me pick out fabric for new curtains in the kids' bedrooms. Mrs. Simmons even sewed them for us, free of charge. Edna also explained to me about Jesus, about his love and care for my children and me. I never knew that before — that Jesus really cares about our needs. We're members of your church now, and I attend one of the Bible studies."

I knew my mouth was open. My Mrs. Simmons suddenly possessed a servant heart. Surely, God performed a miracle when I retired. Or maybe Edna always gave of herself to others, but I only noticed her criticisms of me.

I'm sorry, Lord, for my bitterness against Mrs. Simmons. I'm so glad she befriended Marinda and helped this young woman understand your love. Forgive me, Lord, for not seeing the good in Edna. I focused only on what she did to hurt me. I'm selfish, Lord. I'm sorry.

Marinda told me about her children's school projects, her hopes to plant a vegetable garden in the back yard and her desire to find a teaching position after she graduated. Michael and Sharise started to act a little fidgety, so Marinda stood up. "Let's all tell Reverend G thank you for the drinks and the visit."

Michael, suddenly friendly, shook my hand while Sharise waited behind him to pet Gabriel one last time. Then she came forward and gave me a hug. Marinda also hugged me, then shooed her children out the door. I watched them as they walked down the hall, not realizing that Gabriel had also exited the apartment.

The smell of something delicious traveled from the dining room into the hallway, so I decided to head that way and see what was on the menu. As I turned the corner, I saw the familiar striped tail, like a furry flag, upright and marching toward the front lobby. At least Gabriel wasn't headed for someone's room. I followed him, curious to find out his destination and who he planned to visit today.

As I rounded the corner toward the lobby, the grand piano blocked my view. But I noticed that someone sat in one of the wing chairs near the front door. A beautiful pair of patent leather pumps swung on that someone's leg. Like a pendulum, the leg swung back and forth, keeping time to an invisible rhythm.

I moved closer and saw a hand stroke Gabriel. He rubbed himself against the leg of the chair. It can't possibly be, I thought, so I tiptoed a little closer. Sure enough. Charlotte, the former CEO, sat in the wing chair as she petted my cat with her jeweled left hand. Her face looked softer and something in her eyes seemed to indicate that she truly loved stroking this tortoiseshell cat. Was it a childhood memory or just an unguarded moment? Gabriel seemed content to walk back and forth and beg for Charlotte's touch.

The front door opened and Meredith marched into Cove Creek, her chartreuse tunic accented with a turquoise scarf. Beige pants completed the ensemble and unbelievably, a pair of black patent leather pumps, similar to the ones Charlotte wore. She smiled at her aunt. I hid behind the draperies.

"Where did you find the cat?"

"I don't know," said Charlotte. "I sat down here to wait for you and then this cat rubbed against my leg. He's a pretty thing, don't you think?"

"Indeed, if you like cats. Sorry about being late. Traffic is awful."

"I'm not sure why he's here in the lobby, but he seems well-behaved. I owned a cat once, when I was a child. Did you know that?"

"No, I don't remember you ever telling me about a cat. What breed was it?" Meredith gracefully seated herself in the adjoining wing chair and crossed her feet at the ankles.

"She was Persian," said Charlotte, "with beautiful long white hair. I brushed her every day. I named her Ivory, and she was my best friend. All through grade school, I told her my secrets. She slept with me every night and comforted me when my mother died."

My arm started to itch, and I wondered if the drapery fabric included some type of wool. If my allergy to wool proved true, my nose would soon begin to twitch, followed by a sneeze.

Oh, Lord, this is not a good time for a sneeze. Here I am, hiding in the drapes while Meredith and Charlotte discuss her past and the cat she loved. If Charlotte discovers me eavesdropping, she'll never forgive me. Please do not let me sneeze.

I pinched my nose and planned my exit from the drapes. If I carefully slipped out and called for Gabriel, Charlotte and Meredith might assume I was only looking for my cat — not listening to their personal conversation. It seemed like a good plan.

But as I inched backward, I accidentally backed into a dining room tray and one of the kitchen staff, the loudest of the kitchen staff. Derrick always spoke with a higher volume, probably because some of the residents wore hearing aids. We always knew where Derrick worked. His loud voice preceded him into every room.

"Well, Reverend G," he yelled. "What in the world are you doing in the middle of the curtains? You almost knocked the gelatin off my cart."

"Shh, Derrick. They can hear you all the way downtown to the Dairy Queen. I'm trying to be inconspicuous."

"What? You look like someone just caught you with your hands in the cookie jar. Now come out of there, Reverend G. We can't have our residents hiding in the curtains. Would you like some gelatin?"

"No, thank you, Derrick, no gelatin, but a quieter voice would be nice."

He chuckled to himself as he maneuvered the cart around me and wheeled it toward the dining room. "Hiding in the drapes, that's what. I caught you for sure."

Impossible now to sneak away from Charlotte and her niece. Sure enough, Meredith called out. "Reverend G, nice to see you again. Do you know anything about this cat?"

As I came in full view, Charlotte looked at me and cocked one eyebrow. Probably planned to report me to Roxie for eavesdropping, hiding in the drapes, backing into Derrick's cart or other assorted misdemeanors. Once again, I interrupted Charlotte's conversation and added fuel to her anger.

Gabriel licked his paw and meowed softly. He rubbed against the wing chair leg and begged for more petting. But the softness disappeared from Charlotte's eyes, and the peace of the moment broke. It was time for me to 'fess up.

"As a matter-of-fact, he's my cat and his name is Gabriel. He's kind of become the mascot of Cove Creek. He often visits different residents." Should I mention that most of those residents now lay planted in the Lawton Springs Cemetery? Charlotte probably didn't need to hear that.

"I don't like cats," Meredith said, "but I think Aunt Charlotte enjoyed meeting yours." She stood up. "We're on our way for dinner at a new Italian place downtown. Would you like to join us?"

Charlotte took the cue and also stood. Gabriel jumped into the wing chair. "Meredith, I seriously doubt that the Reverend wants to join us. Besides, I need to speak with you about the details of that last merger. Privately, if you don't mind."

"No problem," I said. "Gabriel and I plan to stay in tonight and watch some *Wheel of Fortune*. But thank you for the invitation and Charlotte, if you ever want to visit my apartment and see Gabriel again, you're more than welcome."

"That would be nice," said Meredith. "Wouldn't it, Aunt Charlotte?"

Gabriel decided at that moment to point his hind leg in the air and groom himself. Charlotte bent down and touched his head one last time before she straightened up and moved toward the door. "We'll see," she said and turned away.

Meredith winked at me and called for Roxie to open the coded door. I picked up Gabriel and walked slowly down the hallway, whispering in his ear. "Good boy. You may have broken the ice cube around Charlotte's heart. Maybe she'll actually visit us and let us be friends."

Gabriel purred and rubbed his face on my arm. I sneezed.

"Roxie, do you have one of those strong allergy pills? I think the wool from the drapes is about to attack me."

chapter 12

"I know it's been a while since I visited you, or called, but there's a good reason for that." Chris sat beside me on the sofa and handed me a small white box with a purple ribbon.

As I reached for the box, my hand shook. Weird. Chris never, ever made me feel nervous, unless this feeling wasn't related to nervousness. Maybe it meant something else, a weird new ailment or a side effect of my dementia. A virus maybe. Unless of course...no, surely not. But why not?

I turned the box over and over, like a giant die, and tried to steady my hands. When did all those brown spots paint themselves on me? My hands looked like those of a really old woman — someone like Mrs. Simmons. Did I have to look like a spotted leopard just because I lived at Cove Creek?

"I've missed you, Chris, but you didn't have to bring me a gift."

"I know, but this is something special. I searched all over Kansas City for just the right one, and finally found it. Downtown, at one of those little boutiques."

I untied the ribbon and broke the Scotch tape on the side of the box. Inside, nestled in tissue paper was an angel, a tortoise-shell cat angel with silver wings. "Oh, Chris, it's perfect. Just like Gabriel. Another angel for my collection. You are the best."

I stood up and walked toward my ètagère, opened the glass door and set the cat angel next to the ordination angel. "You gave me this one, too, on ordination day. Remember?"

"Sure. It was a special day — for both of us. Polly was proud of you, too. She loved you."

"And I loved her. We were a great threesome, foursome, I guess — if you count Frank."

Chris eased off the sofa and stood beside me. His arm encircled my waist. His warm, masculine arm attached to that tall, handsome body so close beside me. "Frank did love you, Tru. But with that awful addiction, he could never be the husband you needed. I'm sorry your married life carried so much pain, sorry you weren't happy."

"If he loved me, he would have tried harder to change. Love means you work hard to keep it. No, Frank chose his path. He had so many chances to defeat the drinking. He could have gone back to AA, stayed with the program and met with his sponsor. He just did not love me enough. He loved the addiction more."

"Can you forgive him, Tru? Have you forgiven him?"

I moved away from Chris and into the kitchen. Suddenly, I felt dizzy and confused. I poured myself some water, then walked past Chris into the living room and sat in my recliner.

"Forgiveness. It's a weird thing, you know. I think I've forgiven Frank, and I feel peace about the whole situation. I ask God to help me truly forgive. Then out of the blue, a memory resurfaces and it all comes back again. Sometimes, I see Frank in Jacob's face, in his gestures, or I hear Frank in Jacob's voice and I want to scream. I don't want Jacob to ever be like his father. Isn't that sad?"

Chris sat across from me and reached for my hand. "Since Polly and I never had children, I can't really understand how that feels. But I empathize with you, and I assure you that Jacob is nothing like his father, at least not in character. Jacob made a vow during high school to never even taste alcohol."

"Really? He never told me that."

"He came to my office and handed me a sheet of paper with his vow typed on it. He signed it and asked me to be his witness."

"Really, Chris? That's wonderful. That makes me so happy. Bless that boy, and bless you for being a substitute father to my son."

Chris leaned back into the sofa. Gabriel jumped next to him and Chris stroked his back. "Frank was my friend as well, Tru. Remember how we all encouraged each other throughout college and graduate school? We were a team. Frank was the finest worship leader I ever met, until the drinking took that away from him. I wanted to help him conquer his addiction, and I wanted to be your friend at the same time. It was a little complicated."

I looked at Chris and for the first time, realized how difficult those years were for him. "I'm sorry, dear friend. I never realized how hard it was for you to help Frank dry out, to pick him up at the bars and drive him home, to watch the effect of Frank's choices on us and explain it all to Polly. What a nightmare!"

Chris shook his head. "Never mind that now. It's all in the past. Friends intervene and help each other. Polly totally understood."

"She was a grand lady. I miss her."

We sat quietly for a while. My mind wandered back to those years when the four of us double dated, when we prayed for each other and spent long summer nights under the stars. We were so young, idealistic and wanting to change the world for Christ. Each of us had our specialties. Chris — the dynamic professor, Polly with her operatic mezzo soprano, Frank and his ability to play several instruments and lead in worship, me with my heart for ministry. We planned to form our own nonprofit evangelistic team, sort of like a Kansas version of the Billy Graham crusades. At one point, we seriously talked about going on the road together to see how far God might lead us.

But shortly after our marriage, Frank started drinking and that ruined everything. We could never depend on him and who wants their worship leader tipsy on Sunday mornings? Then Chris and Polly married and bought a house. They settled into everyday life while I struggled with morning sickness and soon held Jacob in my arms. We flipped through the calendar pages as life marched on, and none of us were ever young again.

Chris broke the silence. "I miss Polly, too, and I'll always love her. But Tru, I love you as well. You've been my confidante, my best friend and the only person I ever talked to about Polly's cancer. I often felt like an adoptive father to Jacob, and I think Frank gratefully let me play that role. You and Jacob are family to me, but Tru, I want more."

"What are you talking about, Chris? What do you mean?" I felt a little dizzy again and leaned back in my chair.

"Hear me out, Tru. Do you remember our picnic on July Fourth?"

"Sure. The fireworks, the children playing all around us, the Star Spangled…whatever it's called…anthem song. It was a nice evening."

"Banner," said Chris. "The Star Spangled Banner."

"Right. Banner." I felt disoriented. Maybe the Sometimer's again. "Do you want more to drink, Chris? All of a sudden, I'm thirsty."

"No, I don't want any more to drink, but I want you to listen to me. That night, Tru, when the kids threw that ball and you practically landed in my lap, I felt something I thought I would never feel again. The fireworks weren't just in the sky, Tru. They exploded in my heart. You're more than a lifelong friend or a sister in Christ. You're my soulmate. I want you. Do you understand what I'm saying?"

The room spun counterclockwise as my heart beat to the rhythm of a Sousa march. I remembered my own feelings that night and wondered why I refused to examine them. Was I afraid or was it another sign of the stupid dementia?

"But Chris, I forget things. You don't want someone who can't even remember what she ate for lunch an hour ago. What did I have for lunch? Do you remember? See, I remember the Fourth of July and even how I felt that night, the fireworks in my own soul. But I can't remember if I ate green beans or cheesecake or gelatin for lunch. Actually, I know it wasn't gelatin, because I don't like that slimy stuff. Never did. Too wiggly. Doesn't stay on the spoon."

"You're avoiding the topic," Chris said with a grin, "no matter how entertaining you are. So how did you feel that night? Did you have the same thoughts? Are we on the same wavelength?"

I suddenly felt the strongest urge to jump out of my chair and fly into those strong arms, to kiss that white beard and run my fingers through that silky hair. But then what? Where would that action lead me? Headed down a path toward demented oblivion, how could I love someone if I forgot those dearest to me? What happened if I gave in to my emotions and then a year from now or even a month from now forgot Chris? I might turn into Bert's Annie or Marie or Grandpa and eventually disintegrate into myself. Would Chris want me then?

Instead of flying across the sofa and smooching on Chris, I started to cry. Chris waited patiently until my tears stopped. "I didn't mean to upset you," he said. "I'm only being honest about my feelings."

I blew my nose and looked into those dear eyes. "I'm not really upset, and these are my honest feelings. They're leaking out all over my face." I cleared my throat and dabbed at the last tears. "I've loved you for a long time, Chris, and more than just a friend. I'm surprised, yet delighted by the strength of my feelings for you. I knew I loved you on the Fourth of July, but truthfully, for much longer than that. I think I avoided dealing with it, because I'm scared. Scared to death to love you with all my heart and then push you away as I become more like a child. I hate this disease and the person I might become. I cannot ask you to live with a demented woman. I love you too much."

Chris nodded. "I know all about your illness, and I'm willing to take the risk. None of us, not even Doc Sanders, knows how this thing will play out. You know, I'm no spring chicken either, but let me love you for however much time we have. Just because we age does not mean we stop living. Let me love you, Tru. Let's embrace life together."

"What are you really saying, Chris? How can we embrace life? Are you proposing, you wonderful man?"

He stood and moved toward the door. "Not yet, because I don't want to shock Jacob and I think we both need time to think about this. I'm only asking for a chance to reach your heart, a chance to let our feelings mature and see what happens. I just want to move from friendship to something deeper. What do you say?"

I smiled and felt a warm glow inside. As I climbed out of the recliner, I petted Gabriel then shanked myself up to my full height. "I say you're a handsome rascal, and if you want to be my boyfriend, then it's okay with me."

In two strides, Chris stood in front of me. His hands caressed my face and his lips brushed against my eyelids. In one glorious movement, we found each other's mouths and all the trust and friendship of the past surged forward into one passionate kiss after another. I had no idea my body was capable of such desire, and I needed all my strength to push Chris away.

He stood in front of me, breathing hard. I felt so dizzy, I fell back into the recliner. "You better go," I said, "before I forget I'm a little old lady with morals."

Chris bent his head back and laughed. His bass guffaw echoed through the room. "Okay, I'll leave, but I'll be back. I promise you, Tru. I'll be back." With a final wave, he walked out the door.

Gabriel's amber eyes seemed to peer into my soul. I put my hands on my hips and looked straight into those orbs. "What are you looking at? Haven't you seen two old people in love?" He responded with a yawn and curled his tail around his body for an afternoon nap.

∽

Sometimes life plants a day in the calendar when everything goes wrong. For some reason, the universe decides to spin backwards and every demon in hell assigns itself to mess with the inhabitants of earth. God always brings good out of the mess, but while we go through it — nothing seems plausible except the chaos.

After breakfast one morning, I followed Gabriel toward his next target. Roxie gave me permission to let him roam, and he seemed to wear a certain look of determination whenever he prepared to pinpoint the next death. On this morning, Gabriel moved quickly down the hallway toward the Memory Care unit, then waited by the door and rubbed his head against the wooden trim.

I motioned to Roxie to punch in the entrance code, and she joined me as we followed Gabriel. Three doors to the right, with his tail erect as the mast on a ship, he followed the nurse's aide into a room. Bright yellow sunflowers stood in a vase in the corner and a crystal cross hung from a chain by the window. It sent rainbow colors to the west wall, reflecting light from the morning sun.

I did not recognize the woman in the bed, but Gabriel seemed ready for duty. He jumped onto the sheets, cuddled up against her and placed his left paw on her hand. Her eyes opened and occasionally, she blinked, but no sound came from her lips as she lay quietly. Roxie walked to the bed and pulled a blanket up to the woman's waist.

"It's a little cool in here, Sandra. There now, isn't that better?" Roxie stroked the thin white hair, then tucked the end of the blanket into the bottom of the bed. The CNA replaced Sandra's water pitcher with a fresh one and left the room.

Still no response from the woman. I looked on the bedside table and saw a picture of a much younger Sandra. She cut a birthday cake and smiled at Doc Sanders. Doc. My doc. So this resident was Doc's beloved Sandra, who lived in Memory Care and suffered from Alzheimer's for so long. According to Gabriel, Sandra's body now gave off the chemicals of death. Within two weeks, she would escape from her disease and the trials of this world. Good news for her, but a deep wound for Doc.

I moved around Roxie and held Sandra's other hand. Roxie bowed her head as I prayed. "Oh, Lord, I see from the pictures that Sandra was a beautiful woman. She's still beautiful in your eyes, and now she's headed home to you. Please let her journey go easy and give comfort to Doc Sanders. We thank you for the assurance of eternity with you. Amen."

"Amen," echoed Roxie. She patted my hand. "I'm going to call Doc. You and Gabriel stay here as long as you like."

I nodded and sat down next to Sandra's bed. Near the birthday picture, a Gideon Bible sat open to Psalm 33. Maybe Sandra's favorite passage. I picked up the Bible and read several sections, "Sing for joy in the Lord, O you righteous ones; praise is becoming to the upright. Give thanks to the Lord… sing praises to Him…sing to Him a new song…all his work is done in faithfulness."

Lord, you are indeed faithful. Help Sandra to sing with joy and praise as you escort her to the beauties of heaven. Give Doc the ability to praise you for the life he and Sandra shared, and even for these past few years when she gave others the opportunity to care for her. You are faithful to the very end, Lord.

Gabriel and I sat there for a while longer. I prayed. Gabriel purred. Then he stood up, stretched his body into a parenthesis shape and jumped off the bed. That seemed to be our cue. I picked him up and carried him into the hallway where we watched a grim-looking Doc Sanders, stride purposefully toward the room to tell his wife good-bye.

∽∾∽

On our way back to my apartment, I heard an awful rack-et from the office area near the front lobby. It sounded like two women arguing about something. Angry, spiteful words. As we passed the head director's office, the door opened and Roxie stood there, shouting into the room. "If you think I'll put up with this type of management any longer, you are sadly mistaken. Not only will I not agree to it, I won't even be here. I quit." She slammed the door, then seemed surprised to see me. I shifted Gabriel to my other arm.

"Oh, my…Roxie…" I started to put a hand on her shoulder, but she brushed past me.

"Goodbye, Reverend G. I'll never forget you." She hurried toward the storage room and soon emerged with two boxes that she carried to her office. Then she slammed the door, obviously wanting to be left alone.

I carried Gabriel to my apartment and put him on the sofa. "Good kitty. I'll be right back." I checked in the mirror to make sure my long braid looked decent, then gulped a swallow of water.

Lord, Roxie is such a great activities director. Everybody loves her, and she's helped me so many times. Can I return the favor and help this dear woman? Should I try to find out what happened? Guide me, please.

No answer. Sometimes God's silence meant that he wanted me to stay away from a situation. But more often, no answer from above meant it was my decision, and he wanted me to use my common sense. This seemed to be the case today, because I felt peace as I stepped into the hallway.

By the time I made it back to Roxie's office, the two boxes stood outside the door filled with books, pictures and some plastic vines. I said a quickie prayer for wisdom, then tapped on the door.

"What?" That stern voice sounded so unlike our Roxie. She obviously wanted to be alone, but I had come this far. I turned the knob and walked in.

"Sorry to bother you, dear, but…would you like a hug?"

Roxie picked up a paper on her desk, crumpled it into a tight ball and threw it into the trash can. "I can't take it anymore. I shouldn't be telling you any of this, but I've had it up to here with this place."

She saluted her forehead, then tossed a magazine into another box. "The powers that be decided to change the vacation policies from two full weeks to PTO — part time off. Do they even realize how many of the staff need a break? A full vacation to relax and recharge our batteries? Do they know how difficult it is to see people like Sandra and Marie and Annie disappear into themselves day by day and week by week? And then they die? Nobody ever leaves here healthy, Reverend G. Nobody."

True words, but I hated to hear Roxie repeat my own thoughts. I was one of those people who disappeared bit by bit each day — headed for the cemetery, worms and dust. Not a pleasant thought, but I understood Roxie's frustration and her need for a long vacation.

"I know, dearie. All of us residents are a sad lot, and we know this is the end of the line. But we appreciate everything you do for us. You're such a trooper, and I don't know what we'll do without you. Please don't quit."

Roxie shook her head. "I have to, as a matter of dignity and principle — to stick up for my staff and our rights. They promised two week vacations when we signed on. I'm overdue for mine, but I can't find time to get away. There's always something more to do, someone else to bury." She grabbed another piece of paper, wadded it tight but this time, missed the trash can.

I thought for a moment. "Maybe it's not the vacation policy as much as the grief of your job. You work so hard, and so much of your work involves death. Such a terrible task — to call family members with the bad news, to let them know death is imminent. Maybe you just need time to grieve the losses, and especially this latest grief — Sandra's impending death. Maybe one or two days away from us would help — a brief R and R."

Roxie sniffed. She tucked a picture frame into another box. "You may be right. I never take time off to grieve." She grabbed a stapler and her desk lamp, then looked up with a slight grin. "Hey, Reverend G. What if we took regular PTO for grief respite? What if they gave us a day every month for mental and emotional leave? Maybe the director would go for that — to relieve some of the stress around here."

"Great idea, Roxie." I loved how this woman rebounded so quickly and came up with new ideas.

"Hmm. I'll think about it, but for now — I intend to pack up and leave. Let the director miss me for a while." She came around her desk and wrapped me in a hug. I smelled her perfume, something with lavender. "Thanks, Reverend G. I'll keep in touch."

"Bless you, Roxie. I'll miss you — for however long it is."

Please, God, comfort Roxie. Lead her in the best direction for her life. Work out this situation for the entire staff. Help us all, Lord, as we give you our grief and let you resolve the stresses of life. I'm grateful that you never take a vacation away from us, no matter how difficult we are.

chapter 13

As I opened the door to my apartment, the phone rang. Jacob started talking when I lifted the receiver. "Mom, are you there? Mom?"

"I'm here, sweet boy. So wonderful to hear your voice. I met the loveliest woman and her children…what are their names? You know, the ones who live in our old house. She told me everything about how you painted and fixed up the house. Oh, my boy — you're so wonderful. What is her name?"

"Marinda, but that's not why I'm calling. Now listen close. A huge thunderstorm is headed for Lawton Springs. Warnings are out everywhere. Be sure you listen to the reports on TV. Do you remember what to do in case of tornadoes?"

"No, not exactly. We don't have a basement here."

"Right, but they'll sound an alarm; then you'll need to get into the hallway. Stay away from windows. Sit down and cover your head. I put a cat carrier in your closet for Gabriel. Remember. Put Gabriel in the carrier and go to the hallway. Okay?"

"You're such a good fellow to remind me. Thank you. I'll watch the news, put Gabriel in the carrier and go to the hallway when the alarm sounds. I've got it. In fact, I'm writing it down on this pad you gave me. You gave it to me, right?"

"Yes, your Don't Forget Pad. That's what you call it."

"Oh, Honey, do you have a minute? I want to talk to you about Chris. Something has happened...."

"No, Mom. I'm on my way home to be with Jess before the storm hits. I'll talk to you later. Now remember, if the alarm sounds — put Gabriel in the carrier and get into the hallway. I love you, Mom."

"Love you, too, sweet Jacob."

Too bad he was in a hurry. I really wanted to talk to him about Chris and the possibility of a future with that hunk of a man. But what should I say? "Chris and I want more of a relationship although the future of my brain cells remains a problem. Marriage and a long-term relationship? Probably out of the question." Really! Who wanted to marry a person whose memory disappeared from one moment to the next?

Now, something I was supposed to do with Gabriel. Oh, yes. Read the instructions on my Don't Forget Pad. Bless that Jacob. Put cat in carrier. Go to hallway — alarm. But first, watch the news.

I turned on the television, then sliced a Granny Smith apple for my mid-morning snack. While I munched, Gabriel joined me on the sofa and we watched the weather reports. There it was — a big red blob of storm headed straight for eastern Kansas, with Lawton Springs right in the center of it. They predicted a hit in forty-three minutes, probably not tornadic but in Kansas — the land of OZ — nobody ever dismissed a weather surprise. The latest warning included hail and some damaging winds, lightning, possibly flash flooding. I hoped Roxie was safely on her way, out of danger with her boxes and pictures.

I checked my Don't Forget Pad again. Listen for the alarm and then put Gabriel in his carrier. But why not get ahead of the game? If I put him in the carrier now, we could be first into the hallway and maybe help some of the other residents. Better to be prepared. Give ourselves plenty of time.

It took a while to accomplish that task. Once I took the carrier out of the closet, Gabriel decided to disappear. I knew he disliked the cat carrier, even though I put a soft towel inside. The last time Jacob took him to the vet for his shots, Gabriel scratched the side of the carrier and howled all the way to the car.

Where is that cat, Lord? Help me find him. I know he hates the confinement of the carrier. Probably reminds him of his trip to the vet and a shot in his rump, but I need him to forget about that now.

I found Gabriel under the bed, huddled in the far corner, his golden eyes turned fierce orange. "Good kitty. Come on, baby, this is for your protection." He slumped farther away from me, back under the headboard. I scootched closer, now completely under the bed. "Gabriel, come on now before I get stuck under here with you. Imagine that report on the television."

"We have a breaking news report from Cove Creek. Reverend G, former associate pastor of the Lawton Springs Community Church expired this evening, under her bed. Family and friends have no explanation other than a tortoiseshell cat missing from the premises."

God, I need your help. Tell this cat to come closer.

"Come on, Gabriel. Cooperate. Really, it will be okay." I cornered him against the wall. Just as he tried to sneak past me, I grabbed his hind leg. He yowled, but there was no way to escape except attached to me as I backed both of us out from under the bed. Then I held him and petted him as he growled a low complaint.

"I'm sorry, sweet kitty, sorry to be so rough with you. But I want you to be safe. It's a good thing we started early. Do you hear those rumbles of thunder?"

The lights flickered twice as I locked Gabriel into his carrier. He yowled again, then turned three circles and settled onto the green towel. "It's just a storm; not the vet. We'll be okay."

I stared out the window as lightning etched a crooked line against the western horizon. The morning sky turned dark gray, and the first peltings of rain splashed against my window pane. The lights flickered again as the weather report interrupted "The Price is Right."

"Heading into Dawson County now with reports of golf ball-sized hail at Conway Lake. Possible power outages and straight line winds. Stay tuned for the latest reports from Action News."

What about lighting a candle, just in case the electricity went out? But then I remembered real candles were never allowed at Cove Creek — something about a fire hazard if we forgot to blow them out.

"No candles, Gabriel. If the lights go out, we'll just wait in the darkness. Where's my flashlight? I'm sure Jacob bought me a flashlight. He thinks of everything. We'll look for it in a minute."

I watched the sky swirl with changing colors and remembered how I taught Jacob to respect Kansas storms. We knelt beside the window seat in our living room and watched the sky darken. How I loved that window seat and all the memories of the books we read there, the prayers we said, the storms we watched develop and fade. Another woman, the one who rented my house, now sat on the window seat with her children. What was her name? Melinda, Melissa, M something. Were her children watching the sky like my little

Jacob all those years ago? Did she try to calm her children and teach them about creation as I taught Jacob?

"Look, Honey. See how God makes the clouds dance across the sky? They change shapes and colors, because he has so much fun rearranging them. Oh, there's a rope of lightning. Do you suppose God twirls a giant lariat in the sky? He whips it around, just to remind us how powerful he is."

"Mommy, look. See the hail? It bounces off the sidewalk."

"Ooh, big ones. Let's pray for the farmers and their crops, dear boy." He bowed his head, and I placed my hand on that dear cowlick as we remembered those who depended on the land for their livelihood. My boy with his tender heart for those in need, even now. He cared for a single mom in that same house where we watched the storms and prayed at the cozy window seat.

The sweetness of memories triggered some tears that rivered down my face as the fury of the storm hit. I saw my reflection in the window glass, my tears blending with the streaming rain. Pebbles of hail ripped through the shrubs as a fresh downpour sheeted against the glass. A giant bolt of lightning hit a tree across the street, and I watched as the bottom limb cracked at its base and hung like a broken arm. Gabriel yowled. The alarm sounded as the lights went out.

∞

With Gabriel's carrier beside me, I sat on the hallway floor and hugged my knees. Staff members ran up and down the hallways, shining their flashlights back and forth so that we could see each other. They occasionally stopped to pat a shoulder or speak to a resident. Derrick shone the flashlight in my eyes and yelled, "You okay, Reverend G? You and that old cat okay?"

I blinked several times. "Yes, Derrick. Thank you. I hear you perfectly."

"Great," he hollered. "I'm off to check on the others."

I heard Bert's voice down another hallway, "When the roll is called up yonder, I'll be there." Good old Bert, who tried to encourage everyone and connect with his Annie through song.

The director's voice echoed from her office. "I'm on my cell phone right now, folks. The generator kicks in within a few minutes. Just be patient. Only a little while longer. We're perfectly safe."

The lights blinked twice, then stayed on. We all cheered. "Hurray," shouted Derrick from around the corner.

I noticed Charlotte at the end of the hallway. Dressed in a sapphire blue suit, she had carried a chair into the hallway. She sat ramrod straight, her legs crossed at the ankles as if she reigned over the rest of us. We huddled on the floor with assorted accessories. Edith held one of her crocheted afghans, a black outline with thousands of other colors in tiny squares. Another resident cuddled with a white teddy bear. Someone else gripped a picture album in her lap.

Take care of my angels, Lord. I forgot about them because I was in such a hurry to grab Gabriel and move to the hallway. Send your real angels, God, to protect us. Help the staff as they take care of us and please, please be with my loved ones. Protect Jacob and Jessie and their wee baby. And Chris. Lord, be with Chris.

Loud thunder booms crashed on top of us. Closer this time. The lady with the teddy bear jumped while Edith clutched her afghan to her chin.

"Aren't you afraid?" Edith asked me.

"Not really. I kind of enjoy storms. They remind me of when my son was little and we watched them from the safety of the house."

"But really," Edith said, "aren't you afraid of what might happen? I wish my children were here."

I scooted closer toward her, dragging Gabriel's carrier along the floor. "You know, Edith, I'm not afraid because I know exactly where I will go if the roof flies off this building and whirls me away."

"I know where you'll go, too. You'll fly into the next county, that's what."

I laughed and touched Edith's hand. "No, dear. I'll fly to heaven and be with Jesus forever."

"And how do you know that for sure? Just because you're a reverend?"

"No. I know it because God says so in the Bible. If we're sorry for our sins and believe that God's son, Jesus, died to make things right — then we go to heaven when we die."

More thunder. A lightning strike that sounded as if it slashed right through the hallway. Edith shuddered.

"Sounds too easy," she said. "Don't we have to do something more to get to heaven? Be good to others all our lives? Never say the wrong thing or never do anything that might hurt someone else?"

"Nope. We can never be perfect enough anyway, no matter how hard we try. The way to heaven is easy, because Jesus already did the hard work. He died for us before we were even born. All we have to do is ask him to forgive us for ignoring him. God loves us and wants us to spend eternity with him. It's that simple."

In all my years of ministry, I never witnessed a fox hole

conversion. But here was Edith, in the hallway of Cove Creek during a Kansas thunderstorm, sitting in her own personal fox hole. Without further prompting, she bowed her gray head over the beautiful afghan and simply said, "I'm sorry, God. If the roof comes off, please take me to heaven. I believe in Jesus."

And in that moment, God saved another soul.

∽

Charlotte stood up and yelled. "Does anyone smell smoke? I'm certain of it. I smell smoke. Fire. There's a fire. Get us out of here."

Edith and I stood and helped each other adjust our stiff knees as the feeling came back into our legs. We moved to either side of the woman with the teddy bear and lifted her arms. Now I smelled it, too. In fact, blue smoke slithered near the ceiling. As a group, we surged toward the front lobby and the double doors.

"Blue smoke," Charlotte cried. "An electrical fire. We've been hit by lightning." She propelled her cane forward and poked the woman in front of her. "Move along. Hurry up. The sprinklers will turn on soon, and then the floor will be wet and slippery. Get out. Move."

Fire alarms sounded all over the building as staff ran from everywhere. Gabriel yowled. Everyone in our hallway moved forward as quickly as possible. Wheelchairs and walkers with their attached residents appeared from other hallways. From the corner of my eye, I saw Bert help two women thread their way through the maze of people. Outside, a siren screamed, decibels higher than the fire alarm.

Ambulance? Fire truck? I could never tell the difference.

Charlotte's prediction about the sprinklers proved true as they swelled open and spewed water all over us. I held Gabriel's carrier closer to my body and tried to keep him as dry as possible. Edith slipped, but grabbed my arm. I pulled her up.

"That was a close one," I said.

"Thank you, God," she replied with a grin.

Just as we approached the front lobby, firemen and police officers rushed in — their helmets and hats wet from the storm outside. They grabbed residents' wheelchairs and raced them through the doors. One fireman hoisted Edith over his shoulder, afghan and all. Someone pushed me from behind, and I stumbled forward. Strong arms caught me, and I looked up into Roxie's concerned face.

"Are you all right, Reverend G?"

"Roxie – you're back or did you ever leave?"

She steered me through the front door. A blast of wind hit me, and I almost dropped Gabriel's carrier. Roxie steadied me. "I was halfway home when the alert came over my cell phone — still programmed into my system for emergency on call. I turned around and hightailed it back here."

"I'm so glad, Roxie. Glad to see you and glad to be out of there. It was a bit scary."

She steered me toward the gazebo. "Wait here. More help will arrive soon and we'll sort this out. The storm is basically over — just a few gusts of wind left. I'm going back inside."

"Be careful," I yelled toward her retreating scrubs.

I sat inside the gazebo and watched as more residents filled the yard. Others joined me on the wooden slats of our temporary shelter. Edith, wrapped in her afghan, sat across from me and chatted with Bert. Gabriel yowled every time a gust of wind moved through. More fire trucks pulled up, along with another ambulance and several police cars. Vans from the TV stations rolled in and journalists poked microphones in front of us.

A reporter asked me how the fire started, and I tried to say something coherent. Then he moved toward Charlotte who stood ramrod straight near the entrance to the circle drive. She spoke into the mike and gestured toward the sky. Charlotte in the spotlight. She seemed to thrive in it.

True to Kansas and its changing weather, the clouds broke apart and the sun again shafted its rays across the horizon. August humidity returned. Edith took off her afghan. "Steamy," she said. Roxie and the director walked out of the building, their arms around each other.

Thank you, God. That relationship problem seems resolved. Thank you for getting us out of Cove Creek safely.

Jacob and Jessie threaded their way through the crowd. Jacob waved, then ran into the gazebo. "Derrick told us you were over here. Oh, Mom, are you okay?" He grabbed my arm and pulled me upright into a hug.

"Of course, dear boy, but I think Gabriel lost one of his nine lives."

Jessie maneuvered closer and peered into the carrier. "He's okay. Just a mad look on his face." She straightened up, and I saw the tiny baby bump under her shirt.

"Oh, Sweetheart. You're starting to show. How exciting!"

Jessie rubbed her tummy and grinned. "Yep. Probably too many late night trips to Ben and Jerry's."

"Chunky Monkey?"

"Of course."

chapter 14

We sat around the TV in Jacob's living room as we sipped drinks and watched reports of the fire. Every local station carried the news. Jacob flipped back and forth with the remote and even found a tiny blurb on a cable news channel.

An empty pizza box sat on the coffee table, filled with our tomato-stained paper plates. Chris sat next to me on the sofa, his arm around me. "I tried to get through the traffic," he said, "as soon as I heard about the fire. But the streets were blocked off and police cars stopped anyone trying to drive through. I finally parked in the hospital lot and walked in. Everything was over by the time I got there."

Jacob nodded. "Yeah, we walked in, too. I tried to get Jess to wait in the car, but she's a stubborn gal." He leaned over and kissed her on the cheek. She winked at me.

The news anchor switched to a video of Cove Creek and the area around the entrance. I stood in the center of the gazebo, my hair in messy gray strands. As I held Gabriel's carrier close, I spoke into the mike. "It was lightning, I guess. A big boom, some blue smoke and then chaos. But our wonderful staff kept everyone quiet, and the firefighters, the police officers — they were incredible. I'm not sure how we got out of the building so quickly. God, of course, protected us."

Chris squeezed my arm. "A minister to the very end, even when she's scared and windblown. My heroine."

I wanted to give him a kiss, but it didn't seem appropriate in front of Jacob, Jessie and my future grandbaby. On the other hand, what better time to smooch your lover than when you've just survived a smoke-filled building and an electrical fire? No one seemed to mind that Chris's arm fit so perfectly around me. He sat so close, I felt his body heat.

Better to wait and let everyone gradually warm to the idea of us old folks in love. Plenty of time later for kisses. I smiled and tried to avoid thoughts about the white-haired hunk next to me.

Jacob flipped to another channel. The video switched from a shattered tree in downtown Lawton Springs to Charlotte. She described the lightning strikes and the blue smoke in great detail, including the fact that she led us all down the hallway to safety. "My compatriots and I calmly made our way to the front door, using the standard procedures. We were never in any real danger; thanks to those of us who kept our wits."

I snickered. "Charlotte is certainly in her element. She sounds like a seasoned journalist." The camera panned the crowd around Charlotte as a tall woman moved toward her.

I sat forward. "Oh, look everybody. There's Charlotte's niece…Mary…or Madeleine…or something like that. It's an M word, I think."

The crowd next to the street parted as Doc Sanders followed a gurney toward the ambulance. A reporter filled in the blanks. "And in another part of the facility, Lawton Springs physician Larry Sanders sat with his ailing wife during the melee. He refused to leave her side, even when the alarm sounded and smoke filled the hallways. Is that right, Doc?"

The microphone steadied in front of Doc Sanders. "She's been my wife all these years. I'm not leaving her now." He stepped into the back of the ambulance, his hand on the metal rim of the gurney.

"Poor Doc," I reported. "Gabriel thinks Sandra's going to heaven soon."

We silently watched the rest of the video as firefighters put out the last of the embers. A black hole gaped in the roof, just over the dining area. Inside video showed the beautiful dining room in shambles, chairs and tables overturned, puddles of water on the tile.

Jacob stretched his legs. "I talked to the director. They'll find places for everyone tonight while they sort things out. It may take a few days, but they already put a tarp on the roof. They start working on the repairs tomorrow. Meanwhile, you're staying with us, Mom, for as long as it takes."

"Thank you, dear ones, for inviting Gabriel and me to stay with you. I cannot imagine going back into my apartment tonight. I'm just so glad no one was hurt. Thank you, Lord."

"Amen," said Chris.

"And amen," added Jacob.

Gabriel napped on a pillow in the corner. He opened one eye, stretched out a striped paw, then settled down for another snooze.

Jessie stood up. "Who wants dessert? Cheesecake or Chunky Monkey ice cream?"

I grinned at my daughter-in-love who carried the next generation in her womb. "I'll take some of both — with blueberries."

MORE GREAT BOOKS FROM CROSSRIVERMEDIA.COM

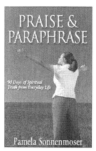

PRAISE & PARAPHRASE
90 Days of Spiritual Truth from Everyday Life
Pamela Sonnenmoser

In Biblical times, Jesus taught his followers through parables — simple stories with a deep spiritual lesson. Author Pamela Sonnenmoser helps you discover how God still uses simple things like loose change, houseplants and turtles to put your focus back on him and change your spiritual perspective.

WHILE THE GIANT IS SLEEPING
Alycia Holston, author / Suzi Stranahan, illustrator

An eagle builds her nest nearby, cars whiz past on the way to visit friends and the Missouri River cuts through the landscape...all while the giant sleeps. In this delightful tale, author Alycia Holston and illustrator Suzi Stranahan introduce you to the Sleeping Giant of Helena, Montana who slumbers while the world continues to grow and change around him.

THE BENEFIT PACKAGE (FALL 2012)
30 Days of God's Goodness from Psalm 103
Tamara Clymer, editor

Based on Psalm 103, The Benefit Package reminds us of all the amazing things our Heavenly Father does for his people. No matter your circumstances or background, God is full of compassion, generous with his mercy, unfailing in his love and powerful in healing. Rediscover God's goodness!

Made in the USA
Charleston, SC
31 August 2012